Books By

KEN BYERLY

INSIDE THE CITADEL

GHOST DANCE

GOOD LOOKING BLOKE AND OTHER STORIES

MOUNTAIN GIRL

RUNNING FREE AND OTHER STORIES

All available, in print and E-Book versions, from amazon,
barnesandnoble.com and other outlets.

INSIDE THE CITADEL

Second Edition

KEN BYERLY

Dr. George Sheehan, "On Running:"
"There is no easy way."

CHAPTER 1

There are people for whom nothing is ever enough. They like storms and mountains. They enjoy sunsets, the wash of waves on a beach. They remember sounds and smells and touches. But they are dragged with such urgency toward some concept of meaning that no sensation, once achieved, is lasting or durable enough. Scott Lehmann was one of these. Scott Lehmann was a beauty lover.

He remembered places and moments and moods. He believed that he tuned in, that he caught the vibrations other missed. It seemed to Scott, as a stockbroker and an unmarried man, that he forever met aspiring investors and single women he could help. And when he felt need, the more beautiful the aspiring investor or the single woman seemed.

He faced two women now, this summer day in mid-Manhattan. The younger one interested him. So did the older one, the casting director at an advertising agency. She wore sneakers and a smock and stood away from the lights.

"Can you act like a football player?"

"I think I can," Scott said. "Is this about football players?" He had come here this morning to audition for a television commercial.

"It's about cars. Actors representing the Green Bay Packers josh and cavort and snap each other with towels in a locker room. Later we see shots of the real Packers on the playing field." At the word "real," she darted a twinkle-glance at her young assistant, virginal in white blouse and white stockings, clasping a clipboard to her chest.

"A car commercial and no women?" Scott smiled at the young assistant. Blonde, ethereal, she looked manacled in this windowless, claustrophobic room.

"Women drive by in a car," the casting director said. "Froth. The point is to show the guys having fun together." She touched her cheek, her face sorted through memories. "Well let's have a look at you." The assistant, dreamy, nodded toward a corner.

Scott gazed at a wall while the two women examined his image on a television monitor screen. He glanced and saw himself: tall, tanned, blue eyes, brown hair. His eyebrows looked heavy.

"Don't look at the monitor. Are you an actor?" The casting director spoke to the monitor, not to him.

"I'm a stockbroker."

"That's interesting. Have you done other commercials?"

"I did a television spot for Lancer Hair Cream."

"How old are you?"

"Twenty-seven."

"Did you actually play football? You look as if you might have."

"I played football in high school and college."

"Where was that?"

"In Illinois," Scott said, glad that she did not ask which college. It was not one of the bigger schools.

"I'm surprised the agency sent you. We don't want real football players. How can you sell stocks and do this too?"

"It's not difficult," Scott said. He saw himself as more than just a purveyor of financial advice. In a good mood, anything seemed possible. He might parachute from dirigibles. He might pen a treatise on collectibles or juggle brightly colored balls.

The assistant strayed, fading from Scott's circle of fun. "Is there a script?" he sought to pull her back. "Lines to read?"

"Not yet," the casting director answered. "Thank you for coming."

Scott hesitated. What might he do to improve his chances? He knew that a roomful of hopefuls awaited beyond the door. He knew that several wore sweatshirts with big football numerals on the back.

Too late. Pitiless, the casting director flung him out into their midst. "Plover," she summoned, and a man wearing a blue YALE sweatband around his forehead leaped to his feet. He looks like an actor, Scott thought, not at all like a football player.

The green feel of June permeated down into the subway as Scott clattered southward. He tried, whooshing past 23rd, to picture Manhattan as it once was, an island rich with forest and ribboned with streams.

The early Dutch settlers hewed down trees and built houses at the bottom of Manhattan Island, near where Scott's brokerage firm now occupied upper floors. Some of the wealthier of those early settlers considered the air unhealthy down there and erected summer cottages in the hills to the north, not far where Scott now lived at 8th Avenue and 20th Street.

Well, they would not recognize the place now. Restless, Scott glanced at headlines in today's *Wall Street Journal* and *New York Times*. He remembered, clattering past Houston Street, that he had lost the phone number of a woman he met on Fire Island, and intended to call today.

Not to worry, he told himself. He must gather more numbers next time.

CHAPTER 2

"Scott, what do you know about Princeton Group?"

"I don't know anything about it, Mrs. Lander. Where is it traded?"

"Over the counter. It's in the paper every Friday."

Scott Lehmann searched out Princeton Group in the Pink Sheets. Happily he found a symbol, PRGP, so he did not have to telephone a trader and wait five minutes on the line to price this one. He punched PRGP into his desktop terminal. "It's under a dollar. It's trading at seventy cents a share, Mrs. Lander."

"A friend from the book club told me about it. What do you think?"

"At seventy cents a share, I'd say it's a gamble. But you never know. I guess all companies have to start somewhere."

"My friend says it will go to five dollars."

"She could say it will go to a hundred. Anybody can say anything."

"I know, but try to find out something about it, will you, Scott?"

Scott Lehmann wanted to think of himself not as an order-taker but as a "financial advisor," a professional who offered ideas and information. He looked up Princeton Group in Standard & Poor's. "It's a plumbing company in New Jersey, Mrs. Lander. They lost money last year."

"Buy me a thousand shares Scott. If I don't and it goes up, my friend will haunt me."

He wrote the order ticket. Three years ago he might have welcomed even this little bit of commission, but now it only dragged his average down. The venerable firm of Tuttle, Osborn & Durkin graded its brokers on the dollar size of the orders they submitted, as well as how many, and the firm would lose money on this one.

"What are you buying?" Barry Kalish asked.

"Princeton Group."

"What do they make? Ivory desks? Ancient scrolls?"

"It's a plumbing company in New Jersey."

Thirty years old, three years older than Scott, Barry Kalish grew up in the Bronx. He had frizzy hair, he spoke with what Scott considered a New York accent, and he had graduated in finance from Columbia University. He and Scott started at Tuttle, Osborn & Durkin on the same day and office manager Walter Cappaletti, a former broker himself, seated them at adjoining desks.

"Where are you from?" Barry asked.

"Illinois."

"The Banks of the Wabash, far away."

"Out there, we think of the Wabash as an Indiana river," Scott said.

"Illinois, Indiana: what's the difference?"

Eight million separate stories, Scott thought, and I draw this guy. He waited for Barry to ask not where, but IF he, Scott, had gone to college. Telephones jangled. The moment passed.

The two of them toiled together in a vast, windowless arena and shared a sales assistant with four other brokers. They stayed late nights and cold-called telephone numbers in Manhattan and its wealthier suburbs and slowly "built their books," as brokers say. Inside the office they swapped ideas. Outside they went their own ways.

The Dow Jones Industrial average, shrunk to below 50 during the Great Depression of the 1930s, climbed slowly through the 1950s and 1960s and in 1969, shortly after Scott and Barry arrived on Wall Street, made its first run at 1000. It just missed then, and it had just missed several times since. Now, in the summer of 1972, two new World Trade Center towers climbed toward the sky and the Dow Jones challenged 1000 again.

Scott's telephone rang. "Where is Rico Chemical?" asked Ingrid Henson, executive secretary at ZaneCorp, an international metals firm headquartered uptown on Park Avenue.

Scott punched up the symbol, RCO. "Forty-four and a half, Ingrid. Want me to check and see what our analyst thinks?"

"No need on this one, Scott; Mr. Crosland heard about it at a charity ball. I want you to buy him a thousand shares. Buy Mr. Irvin five hundred, also at the market, and see if you can get me two hundred at forty-four and a half, okay?"

Scott wrote the buy tickets, colored blue to distinguish them from red sell tickets. He stuffed the orders into a pneumatic tube and zoomed them away. These slips of paper would produce about $900 in commissions for Tuttle, Osborn & Durkin and he would keep about a third of that.

One college summer he shoveled sand into a concrete mixer for $7.50 an hour. It took him ten eight-hour days of shoveling sand to earn, before taxes, about $300. Today he had just made that much in a minute. Scott had to remind himself sometimes that this was real money.

Yellow-green stock symbols skittered across his desktop terminal. 500 RCO glided by, several 100s and then a block of 1000. My doing, Scott thought. He fought a temptation to float along with the numbers.

He thought back. The ZaneCorp accounts came easily, in contrast to the repeated mailings and phone calls it took to acquire most of his clients. Scott cold-called ZaneCorp, someone referred him to Ingrid Henson, they talked, and she opened three accounts within the week. She told him later that she chose him because she liked his voice on the telephone.

Barry Kalish's head popped above the partition that separated their desks. "What's up?"

"Same old stuff," Scott said. Casually he flipped face-up a buy order for one million shares of General Motors that he held in waiting for a moment like this.

"Funny," Barry said, and, as if to punctuate this instant in history, a pneumatic tube pounded home bearing order confirmations. Crosland and Irvin bought RCO at forty-four and five-eighths, Ingrid at forty-four and a half. Scott called and read her the prices. It pleased him, and he knew it pleased her, that she paid twelve and a half cents a share less than her two ZaneCorp chieftains.

Scott worked his telephone, suggesting buy this, sell that, talking with customers. Some followed his advice. Many didn't. "Where's Chromos Technology today?" a dentist asked.

Scott punched at his terminal. "Twenty-one and an eighth."

"Buy me two hundred shares at nineteen and a half, okay? Day order only."

"Christ, Dan, there's only thirty minutes left," Scott said. "Chromos won't drop to nineteen and a half unless the company president commits suicide or Russia attacks. Why don't you come up a little?" Dan usually priced his buy orders way below market, and as a result rarely bought anything.

"I've got a hunch on this one, Scott."

Scott entered the order. Nothing came of it, but he enjoyed a profitable day. He spun in his swivel chair and imagined himself in a private office with a huge picture window. He'd sit above the world and gaze down at passing ships in New York harbor. He'd ponder the two rising World Trade Center towers and announce to the office whenever tiny-dot workmen completed another floor.

Yellow-green symbols and numbers skittered across his computer screen. Scott watched, entranced at this restless seething. The stock market became for him at moments like this a woman to charm and possess. Already he looked forward to tomorrow morning, to that transitory instant when symbols and numbers flickered, began to move, gathered speed.

Scott Lehmann savored the feeling that every day when the stock market opened he cracked the seal on a brand new deck of cards.

CHAPTER 3

Art Levin, five-foot-nine city planner, brushed his black hair straight back. He wore glasses, jeans, a suede vest and thick leather laces wrapped around each wrist. "Lash Storm," he greeted Scott, who approached, suit jacket slung over his shoulder, through the Friday afternoon heat and tumult of the lower level at Penn Station.

"Salut, Lamont Gramercy Cranston."

"Flail the tocsin, shout 'hooray;' we toiled five days, tis time to play." Art spoke distinctly, as if for any lucky passerby to hear, and his eyes sparked with creative knowing.

"Lucky moment, week's labor done; time for frolic, time for fun." Scott had composed his couplet on the subway uptown to the train station. This creative rhyming erupted during their coed beach house's opening weekend in May. Art's nimble mind triggered Scott's competitive flair – now they dueled to see who could top the other.

A gate swung wide, they surged to a train platform in a crush of commuters and summer weekenders. "It begins," Scott said, as he would say every two weeks all summer. Train doors parted, they pushed toward the bar car.

They purchased cups of ice for a dollar. Scott produced a pint of Scotch from his weekend bag and carefully poured. Art tasted, nodded, looked around for an audience. "Art laughs, Art sings; he'll be ready when the bell rings." Two women in blazers standing nearby exchanged a cautious glance.

Art introduced Scott as, "Lash Storm, test pilot."

"Lamont Gramercy Cranston, philanthropist," Scott presented his friend. "The Cranston Pavilion at Columbia; surely you know it." He edged closer to the taller of the two women.

"I race formula four stock cars," she said.

"I'm president of a small Latin American country," her friend said.

Scott liked these two, but he and Art changed trains at Jamaica in Queens. Art rhymed for a cluster of school girls, who promptly turned their backs and communed among themselves like birds along a highway who no longer raise their heads at passing cars.

The two men shared a taxi to the waterfront with several others in Patchogue halfway out the south shore of Long Island. A ferry boat rocked at anchor and they hurried up a ramp to the top deck.

Benches filled. A motor coughed and churned. The ferry jerked and eased past phlegmatic gulls perched on poles. The horizon behind reddened with sunset and New York and the work week fell away. Someone strummed a guitar. The world smelled of salt and sea. The weekend began.

Scott eyed the people around him in a spasm of goodwill. Everything seemed possible crossing Great South Bay.

Fire Island took shape ahead, a long, thin barrier between the bay and the Atlantic Ocean, a smudge against a blue-black sky. The lights of Davis Park separated from each other and grew more distinct as the ferry drove toward them across the water. Summer houses appeared, dunes, scraggly trees. The ferry slowed and bumped against a pier littered with grocery boxes and little red wagons.

"Consarned wagons." Scott playfully kicked at one. People used them to trundle groceries to their houses and every Friday they cluttered the pier shoulder to little red shoulder.

He and Art clomped inland on one of the narrow, wooden walks that sliced patterns across the sand. Gentle gaslights glowed inside clapboard houses, no two the same. Shadows moved, voices sounded. Scott heard beyond the barrier dune the crash of the Atlantic Ocean.

The first ads had appeared in March: "Davis Park – a few 1/2 shares left, coed house. Exciting minds looking for contrib. We're selective – what can you offer?"

Scott attended a hopefuls party and survived the selection voting. Most houses soon filled their quotas, but even now in June an occasional ad still surfaced in the city: "Clearance sale – Davis Park. Male and female 1/2 shares. Long season."

They approached a ramp extending from the sun deck of an octagonal, many-windowed house raised on stilts driven into the sand. A glass door dominated the ocean side and Scott saw several of their housemates lounged along the bar inside. Larry Silverman held sway as they entered, "...too many characters, and most of them men..."

"What? Which?" Scott asked.

"War and Peace."

"What about Natasha? You can't help but fall in love with Natasha." Scott remained eager to establish his credentials as an exciting mind with much to offer.

"Bother Natasha," Larry Silverman said.

"I saw the movie. I never read the book." Marlene Miller stroked her long, dark hair. "Where's our grocery box? Where's our gin?"

"I looked. I don't think the grocery boat came yet," Scott said.

Barbara Feldstein, eyes big and brown behind thick glasses, mounted the stairs from bedrooms below. "Well, Arthur," she said, "what elderly tenant's heart did you break today?"

"Unfair," Art Levin said. "You know whose side I'm on."

All week long back in the boroughs he inspected low-income apartments for the City of New York. Barbara Feldstein taught at a junior high school in Scarsdale. Larry Silverman and Marlene Miller worked at advertising agencies. All, like Scott, lived in

Manhattan apartments, and paid several hundred dollars for the opportunity to live in this summer house every other weekend until September. This was their third weekend together. A different group arrived on alternate weekends.

Barbara touched one of Art Levin's leather wrist shoelaces as if examining a primitive sculpture. "Are these for archery practice?"

"No." Art looked around for help.

"Our groceries ought to have arrived by now," Marlene Miller said.

"I'll go," Scott said. This should help him avoid washing dishes. He thunked along wooden walks and roamed the cluttered pier until he found a box marked "M. Miller." She had called from the city earlier that day to order and a merchant in Patchogue dispatched their wares across Great South Bay on a business boat.

Scott searched for their house wagon, couldn't find it. It was almost dark. Conspiratorial, a beachcomber Jesse James, he kidnapped another little red wagon and trundled their food and liquor home.

He changed from his workaday suit to jeans and white shirt in a downstairs bedroom with two bunks for guys. Marlene Miller glanced from the bathroom across the hall where she applied makeup. "Boat crowded?" she asked.

"Not bad." Scott watched Marlene paste another false eyelash into place. New York women: they did everything but go to the toilet in front of you without a hint of embarrassment. He wondered, as the only non-Jew in the house – the "token goy," as Larry Silverman put it – if ethnicity shaped behavior. For instance, he left the water running while he brushed his teeth. He felt he had much to learn.

Scott and the others, except Barbara Feldstein, who resisted bars and casual trolling, sallied forth on a wooden walk. Art still wore his suede vest, but now with his chest bare underneath. Larry had donned a denim jacket. He and Art walked in front talking baseball.

Scott fell in next to Marlene, an angel of decadence in a tight, black jumpsuit. She flashed him a glance. "So, you liked Natasha?" Beyond the dune, the ocean made long cracking sounds.

"I did. Yes."

"You prefer them innocent?"

"Well..." Scott hesitated.

"I get off on Vronsky in *Anna Karenina*," Marlene said.

The Casino, an edifice of weathered and unpainted wood, balanced on the highest point of the barrier dune. Music reverberated and the place seemed to shake. Heat blasted from its front door.

Aretha Franklin's *Respect* jolted from the jukebox. Scott and Marlene edged into a writhing mass on the dance floor and elbowed for space. She tossed her hair and made swimming moves with her arms. Scott slid closer, admiring.

Larry Silverman cut in. Scott, stranded, recalled a woman he knew who questioned the inner strength of men who danced with females from their own house. He wondered if right now, somewhere in this crowd, she observed and knowingly shook her head. Boldly he pushed to the bar and called for a gin and tonic, not as confident as he pretended. This wasn't a country dance back in Illinois near the terminal moraine.

Art Levin, Sherlock Holmes pipe in one hand, a drink in the other, prospected a young woman. Scott glanced around for strays. "Here I am, what have you got to offer?" – these women arrived prepared to negotiate. He wanted to meet many, and had, but lately the pace had slowed.

A tall brunette, a Cleopatra snake ornament coiled on her arm, brushed past. She glanced back, caught his eye, and swung through a screen door onto a balcony over the ocean.

Scott stepped out on the balcony and leaned next to her at a railing. "Nice night," he said. The moon shone on the water and as a wave retreated it looked as if somebody rolled a silver blanket back toward the sea.

She studied him through eyelashes as thick as spider's legs. "It is a nice night," she said.

"I think I met you last winter skiing at Mount Snow." Viewing her up close, suddenly Scott thought he had.

"Not me," she said. "I'm a klutz on the slopes. I like warm water. Every winter I plan to go hike the Grand Canyon and every winter I wind up in a beachfront hotel in San Juan. Are you in the house with Manny Gold?"

"I'm with Art Levin and Larry Silverman."

"I'm Barbara Fine. What's your name?"

"Scott Bernstein," he said.

She looked him up and down. "You're not from New York, Scott Bernstein."

"I'm sorry," he said. "I don't know why I said that. I'm Scott Lehmann and I'm a Lutheran from the great plains."

"I thought you were a Smith or a Jones or something like that. If I wanted a Bernstein I would look for a Bernstein. We've a house full of Bernsteins."

"I misjudged you, Barbara Fine."

A man called from below and she, hand poised as if to drive home an observation, patted Scott on the shoulder instead. "Happy hunting," she said, and danced down the stairs.

Scott talked with other women, recorded a phone number or two, but achieved no lasting connection. The Casino closed and acres of sand gleamed in the moonlight. Embarrassed at leaving alone, he walked toward his house along the beach.

The ocean thundered. Scott stopped to stare up at the stars. Why had he identified himself to Barbara Fine as Jewish rather than a country boy from Grange, Illinois? Had he told the truth, would she have expected him to break whiskey bottles or something? He felt uncomfortable at his subterfuge and wondered why he attempted it. Maybe the women in his house voted him in because they viewed him as some sort of reclamation project. The men, he suspected, claimed him to improve their house touch football team.

The sun shone in the morning, the ocean sparkled, and Scott and the guys played touch football on the beach. Left-handed Larry Silverman filled the air with touchdown passes, Scott his favorite target. Art Levin sprinted toward Europe and dived to make a miraculous catch. "Aerial circus! Aerial circus!" he shouted, sand on his face. Quarterback Larry, paunchy, balding, smiled his crooked grin.

Blanket clusters formed and dissolved. Women worked cross-word puzzles, read novels; joggers passed in baseball caps. Every hour or two Scott and whoever else he could cajole sprinted into the ocean, swam lustily back and forth and bobbed with seagulls between the waves.

Shadows lengthened, the beach began to empty. Sunburned people carried beach chairs and blankets away. Here, there, an almost palpable anticipation flared. The Saturday Sixish beckoned.

Scott, home, mixed gin and tonic and slices of lime in a blue enamel coffeepot. Outside on wooden walks streams of brightly dressed people flowed from houses on stilts toward an otherwise unremarkable stretch of sand along Great South Bay.

Marlene Miller sported the blue and white stripes and striped cap of a railroad engineer, Art Levin the plaid shorts and football jersey of a housing inspector at leisure. Scott and Larry Silverman dueled in dullness with Bermuda shorts and polo shirts, though Scott did carry the blue enamel coffee pot. Barbara Feldstein once more stayed home.

People who had shared blankets two hours ago on the beach embraced as if they had not seen each other for weeks. "Look who's here!" "Sandy!" "Maxine!" Upwardly mobile city dwellers milled on a sandy, open space and more arrived by the minute.

"It's a meat market," Marlene Miller said. "Why don't they just say, 'let's fuck.'"

Scott held tightly to his blue coffee pot and periodically refilled his own and his housemates' glasses. He edged through conversations toward the water. Little waves lapped at his feet and across Great South Bay a tired red sun smoldered.

"What's in the coffee pot?" a woman asked.

"Rhubarb squeezings and melancholy." Scott noted chiseled cheekbones, brown eyes flecked with gold. This could be The One, he thought, but, lo, a man in a white hat led her away.

Scott wandered in search of greatness. Marlene Miller sprawled on the sand with a man in a red sweater. Scott offered the coffee pot and Marlene extended her glass. She had removed her sandals and bare feet extended. She wiggled her toes.

A huge red sun embraced the earth and bloodied the horizon. A lone ferry sliced across Great South Bay. Scott poured the last of his coffee pot elixir into his own glass. He saw Barbara Fine, a reminder of his attempt at identity subterfuge last night, barefoot on the sand with a swarthy man in gold chains and shirt open to the navel. Scott caught her eye, she lifted her glass.

Clumps of people slid away. Scott sat down on the board-walk, legs dangling, and clutched his empty coffee pot. No crowd would gather here tomorrow or the next day or the day after that, he thought. Shreds of tattered paper might rattle past in the wind. Then next Saturday, and the Saturday after that, it would all happen again.

Scott Lehmann rose to go. Darkness smoothed the day's imperfections, he noted. The surrounding sweep of trampled sand appeared dappled, as after a gentle rain.

CHAPTER 4

The windows of Scott's sixth-floor corner apartment at Twentieth Street and Eighth Avenue faced north and east. The Empire State Building dominated his view; his mountain, he thought, a never-ending treat after those pie-plate plains of southern Illinois.

Scott descended his elevator, walked to Twenty-Third Street and bounded down subway stairs. Good, got a seat. He scanned the front pages of newspapers and thought back to his weekend at Davis Park. No promising phone numbers. Had he become too cautious, he wondered?

He climbed the subway stairs to Rector Street, arched his neck and peered upward at the spires of the new World Trade Center. Look at that: the north tower appeared to glide westward against clouds that oddly stood still. This tower had attained its final height and tenants already occupied lower floors. The south tower, close by, only about two-thirds as high, continued to rise at the rate of about two floors a week.

Scott climbed the hill past the metal fence of Trinity Church yard and the grave of Alexander Hamilton. He imagined Hamilton whispering, "Strong money, strong bank" in one

George Washington ear, Thomas Jefferson intoning, "Gentleman farmer" in the other.

Appropriately, Hamilton reposed here now, amid ledgers and brokerage houses, Jefferson in the rural Virginia hills.

Scott walked up Broadway to Wall Street. It still impressed him, after three years, that he worked just around the corner from the New York Stock Exchange. An elevator sped him to the 24th floor and his fingers twitched, eager for the chase. Almost time to crack that new deck of cards.

A young woman he had never seen before sat at a desk near his. She wore high heels and a gossamer blouse and her dark hair framed bee-stung lips. "Nice weekend?" she asked.

"The sun shone," Scott said. Noting her questioning lift of eyebrow, he added, "I'm Scott and I was at a beach house on Fire Island." Barry Kalish walked in and he too looked perplexed at this new person. She extended her hand and introduced herself as Monica Corbin. Originally from Waycross, Georgia, she had graduated this month from Bennington College in Vermont, a liberal arts bastion she attended on an academic scholarship. Walter Cappaletti had assigned her to Scott and Barry as their sales assistant.

"He asked me to point the two of you toward his office. 'As soon as they arrive' – he was explicit about that."

Walter grinned as they entered. "Yes, yes," Scott and Barry agreed.

"She tested high," Walter said. "She wants to become a broker herself. I promised you a sales assistant; here she is. You two continue to grow your businesses, I think we can find you private offices down the road."

This day begins well, Scott thought. Walter rose, closed his door and lowered his voice. "She's part black," he said. "Monica, I mean. I mention this only to avoid embarrassment if the subject ever arises. I don't know how much she is of this or how much she is of that and I don't care. As you can see, she seems to have inherited the best from all sides."

Scott and Barry returned to their desks. Monica balanced on a chair, stretching, stretching, for something on a shelf above.

"Envelopes?" Scott asked.

"Please. The number tens."

He darted with the quickness of a mongoose and pulled down a batch. "So, how do you like the West Side?" he asked. Walter said Monica had rented an efficiency in the West Eighties.

"It's a long subway ride. Where do you guys live?"

"I'm on East Thirty-Three," Barry said.

"I'm on West Twenty," Scott said. "Barry and I started here on the same day three years ago."

"Three years: you've done well then." Monica stood with her hands on her hips. "Later, if either of you makes some prospecting calls, I'd love to listen in, if you don't mind."

"Good idea," Scott said. He had not intended to call prospects today, but now decided he should.

George Rogalski entered toting a briefcase, newspapers and a styrofoam cup of coffee. "Morning, guys." He stopped and cocked his head at Monica. Past 50, George still wore his hair in a crewcut. He commuted every day from New Jersey and he possessed a sales assistant all his own.

Scott introduced him to Monica and brusquely George shook hands. "Any of you catch *Night of the Trifids*?" He liked science fiction movies.

"Missed it, darn," Scott said.

"George, there's a good one on tonight you ought to see," Barry said, "*Good Times at Wilmot High*."

"Saw it, found it wanting." George retreated into his private office where he would sit all day grimacing, complaining, making money, emerging occasionally to view with alarm.

"Drat, the Golden Falcon," Barry said. Blond Bruce Stanton, child of privilege, bounded toward them through the cubicles.

Bruce aimed straight for Monica. "Hello. Saw you earlier. Meant to introduce myself."

"Them whiffenpoofs make bad sounds," Barry said. The Golden Falcon had graduated from Yale.

"Basketball tomorrow?" Scott sought to blunt Bruce's brilliance. He had sensed Bruce's reluctance to participate in basketball, and thus he continually suggested a game.

"I'll play basketball after you play me a game of squash."

"Squash," Barry said, exploring all the strangeness in the word. "Squash."

"It's not a game for nambies, my friends," Bruce said. Monica looked from one to the other. All this for her, Scott thought. I should be on the telephone selling.

Bruce departed. The market opened; yellow-green numbers raced past on their computer screens. "Scott, Mr. Polinsky," Monica called.

"Good morning, Scott. You had a nice weekend? Today I want you to buy me three hundred Conrad Computer."

"Will do. It's at twenty-three and a half, Mr.Polinsky." Scott wrote the buy ticket and whooshed it away. Mr. Polinsky owned a hardware store on Staten island and liked to make his own decisions. Scott had gotten his name from a prospect list and called.

"Lehman. Is that Jewish?" Mr. Polinsky asked.

"No. Double N. My father's parents emigrated from Germany."

"That's right, there's not a lot of Jewish boys named Scott." Even so, next time Scott called Mr. Polinsky opened an account.

"Store owner, probably works seven days a week," Scott said to Barry Kalish. "It always surprises me when these city guys decide to trust me."

"They think you're too dumb to cheat."

"Or sense a deeper wisdom." Scott strolled outside noon hour and sat on the steps of the Federal Building across Wall Street from the New York Stock Exchange. The sun soothed and he watched office girls stride by. But in a few minutes he wondered what the market was doing, so he bought a cup of tea and an apple raisin muffin and returned upstairs.

George Rogalski dozed in his chair behind his open office door. Scott caught Barry's eye and they crept in and sang together, to the tune of *The Streets of Laredo*, "I'm a sugar trader and I know I've done wrong. I went short when I should have gone long..."

George opened his eyes and peered at them. He liked to speculate in commodities and he had recently, with some fanfare, sold ten sugar contracts short. Sugar had risen in price and

George had lost money. He assumed a hurt look. "Those who can't do criticize," he said.

Barry took a phone call. Scott gazed out George's vast windows. Feather clouds floated in a summer sky and a flash of sun skittered across New York Harbor. "George, you think the Dow will make it through a thousand this time?" Scott sought to make amends for the sugar trader song, so he threw the Old Timer a pontification bone.

George stared past the new trade center towers toward Bermuda, the South Atlantic and the Tropic of Capricorn, his face etched with the sorrows of the ages. "Profits implode," George said. "The government's budget deficit explodes. Speculation races endemic." His expression softened. "Let the bulls run when they want to run," he said. "Don't fight the tape, Scott, my boy. Don't fight the tape."

Scott nodded sagely, but what had George said? He returned to his desk and telephoned clients on a bond offering, hoping to generate other business in stocks and mutual funds. He became aware as he worked that Monica Corbin crossed her legs and that on one swinging foot a high heeled shoe slipped on and off, on and off.

His telephone rang. She glanced toward him. "Brent Hall, line two."

"Cool, for June, not much wind," Brent began, and Scott knew where this conversation tended. Brent worked as a textbook editor and the two of them played basketball either indoors or outdoors at least twice a week.

"I didn't bring my stuff today," Scott said. "How about tomorrow at Leroy Street?"

"I'll be there."

"The Bank's on the phone," Monica Corbin called. Already she used Scott's code name for Ingrid Henson.

He reeled off quotes on Rico Chemical and other stocks. Ingrid cut in. "Does art interest you. Scott?"

"I like art," he said.

"Rembrandts and other old masters, paintings on loan from the Hermitage in Leningrad, will be shown at a special exhibit

Friday night at a gallery on Fifty-Seventh Street. ZaneCorp is a sponsor, along with other corporations who do business with Russia; I can get you a pass."

"Will you be there?"

"No, but I can leave your name at the door."

"I'd like that, Ingrid. It's my off-weekend at Fire Island."

"Got a date? Want two passes?"

"Thanks," Scott said. "One will do this time."

He totaled his commissions when the market closed, as he did at the end of every working day. He signaled Monica and pretended to make a prospecting call. She clicked on to the line. "Mr. Client," Scott intoned, "if you do what you're told, your pockets will be filled with silver and gold."

Monica appeared startled, and then she realized nobody listened on the other end. Scott chuckled. He signaled again. "Ready? This is for real." He called a prospect he had spoken to before, and who had seemed friendly.

Splendid coincidence, the man chose this moment to open an account. Monica beamed and flashed him thumbs up.

CHAPTER 5

Scott Lehmann gripped newspapers in one hand, an airline bag of gym clothes in the other and leaned against a pole, rocking with the motion of the subway train. An old man slumped in a seat across the aisle, apparently asleep. He wore no shoes or socks and his ankles looked dirty.

Not good: weary old vagrants barefoot and broke while the city above groaned with money. Scott tried to picture this old man as a boy with a dog and a baseball. He saw corn fields, a front porch swing, a swimming hole down by the creek. He liked to study old folks and imagine their lives and how they looked when they were young.

He bought a cup of "regular" coffee to go (sugar, a dash of milk) and carried it up to his office, an extra snap to his step today. Monica Corbin did not disappoint. She wore a wide leather belt, a see-through red blouse and crimson high heels.

An analyst on the squawk box touted the high dividend yield of stock offer today by a Rhode Island electric utility. Monica offered a list of Brown University graduates who lived in the New York City area to Barry and Scott. Barry passed. Scott telephoned graduates of the Providence, Rhode Island school one-by-one, seeking new accounts as well as to peddle the utility stock. He opened two new accounts and worked the list again in the afternoon.

He stood to stretch, glanced into George Rogalski's office and saw to his surprise that a lightning storm raged outside. George motioned him in to see.

The two men stood transfixed. One jagged flash succeeded another. Rain streaked the raw steel of naked girders jutting from another floor-in-progress atop the south tower of the World Trade Center. Streams of water spurted from mysterious apertures.

"Lightning hit it yet?" Scott asked.

"If it did, I didn't see it," George said.

"Wow! That one looked close!" The two men watched, hopeful, but the lightning muttered and died, a shard of sun cut through.

Pavement still steamed later that afternoon as Scott carried his bag of gym clothes down the hill to the Rector Street Subway Station. He rode a train north and climbed exit stairs to Hudson Street.

It was if he had taken the wrong train and gotten off in Smog City. Fire escapes dangled from old buildings, nobody walked on the sidewalks, and Seventh Avenue reeked of bumper-to-bumper trucks impatient to enter the Holland Tunnel.

Scott approached the dingy, fortress-like city gymnasium on Leroy Street. All its doors looked like back doors and bars barricaded the windows. A stranger would never guess at the nearness of trendy Greenwich Village and the glory of gentle trees and townhouses around the corner on St. Luke's Place.

Scott entered an unmarked door, descended dank stairs and instantly felt at home. He loved that sloppy, rank locker room smell you never forget if you play sports and go to school in America.

He changed to shorts, t-shirt and hightop basketball shoes and climbed the ancient, circular metal staircase to the basketball court above. A polished floor shone in the light from high windows. Brent Hall shot baskets at one end while at the other end a gaggle of neighborhood kids screamed and cursed at each other.

Scott and Brent shot baskets without speaking. Both had played basketball for their little colleges, Brent in Oklahoma, Scott in Illinois. Their shoes squeaked on the gleaming floor. "Walt Frazier" – Brent named a player on the New York Knicks – and lofted a Frazier-like floater. "Bill Bradley," Scott said, and launched an outside jumper. The ball coming off his fingertips felt like pebbled gold.

The kids left. It got quiet. Brent lazed in an underhanded layup. "Remember," he said, "when you were a kid, how fun it was to sneak into the gym and shoot on the glass backboards?" Scott saw him actually remembering.

Other men climbed from the locker room in torn off sweatshirts, worn hightops, bearded men, bald men, all shapes, colors, sizes. Some subwayed down from Harlem. Some, like Scott and Brent, lived close enough to walk from their apartments. Some said that the bald guy had played at Ohio State and that several others played in prison. It didn't matter. All that mattered at the Leroy Street gym was that you came to play the game.

They chose sides and as usual Scott and Brent managed to wind up on the same team. Brent brought the ball down. Scott played underneath. Both could shoot, and they had played together so often they anticipated each other's moves.

"Who's got the Big Man?" Scott knew that was him. He stood six-two, not big at all in basketball, but the blacks designated whoever played the pivot, "Big Man."

"Whoa, now. Easy, Jim." Jim was Brent. The blacks called some of the white players, "Jim," and here in the city of eight million stories their idiom defined the game.

Scott intercepted a pass. The flow reversed. "Watch his left-hand hook," someone called.

"Shit. What left-hand hook?"

Scott felt pressure on his right. He spun the other way and nailed it with his left hand.

"You traveled," the man guarding him said. "He traveled," he protested to all who could hear.

Too late. Life hurried on.

Brent pumped one off the glass and in. Another shot floated up. The flow tumbled the other way. Scott exulted. He felt young and strong. He could not believe that someday he might grow too old.

His team lost. Winners stayed and losers stood so he and Brent leaned against the wall and watched the survivors in action.

"See, he always fakes twice."

"Let him shoot from out there."

"He won't drive. You can crowd him." They watched the action as if nothing mattered more than which team scored five baskets first.

They won next time out, and continued on to win four in a row. When they lost, they waited to play again. Eventually, sweaty, happy-tired, they clomped down the stairs.

Red-haired Brent soaked in a shower, as sunburned on his face, neck and wrists as a Dust Bowl farmer. His family had moved from Oklahoma to California, his father had died, his mother lived with a younger daughter somewhere. "Good one," he commented, meaning tonight's basketball in general.

Scott grunted an assent through steam and splash. He felt purged after two hours of running and sweating.

"What's that you say? You WILL go to more TV commercial auditions?"

"No, that's over," Scott said. "It takes too much time. Stock market might move twenty points while I sit around waiting my turn." He tested his friend, hoping Brent would urge him to keep trying.

Brent did not. They strolled up Seventh Avenue. Yesterday had been the longest day of the year and a golden band of light lingered over New Jersey.

"Caught *The Gunfighter* on TV last night," said Scott, a connoisseur of the sagebrush genre. "Gregory Peck broods in dusty bars, there's a woman, one chance left. Kid in search of a reputation shoots him in the back."

"The old West was not a happy place," Brent said.

They settled themselves in a talkers' bar near Sheridan Square, nudged their bags of basketball gear under the table and ordered steamer clams and a pitcher of beer. Brent had recently read some James Joyce short stories and he described them as "crisp and as clean as new rope."

Scott nodded. Brent, a textbook editor, had a touch for a phrase. "What's doing in educational publishing?" he asked.

"French is hot. We call the colleges, offer the profs 'consulting fees' if they choose our book."

A woman in a peasant blouse and sandals passed their table. Brent looked after her. "I met a contender Saturday," he said.

"Tell me."

"At a party. She's a speech therapist, tall, sporty. She's Catholic from Queens."

"Good looking?"

"Oh yes," said Brent, a strayed Baptist himself.

"Call her yet?" Scott felt his friend needed prodding at times.

"I will."

"Ask her to something cerebral."

"Eugene O'Neill. I'm ahead of you there. I think it was my James Joyce riff that piqued her interest."

They discussed the New York Knicks and the books of John Steinbeck. Brent's sunburned face and his earnestness reminded Scott of Henry Fonda as Tom Joad in the movie *Grapes of Wrath*.

They strolled up Seventh Avenue, the Empire State Building looming ahead. "Ain't life grand," Scott quoted a line from the movie, *Bonnie and Clyde*.

Brent grinned. "If we're prepared to receive it." He turned left toward his apartment on West Eleventh. Scott walked on north toward Twentieth.

CHAPTER 6

An animal in the wild first of all notices movement. Scott Lehmann noted the glide of black stockings and a blue dress into the periphery of his field of vision.

He had changed at his apartment to white shirt, tie and blazer and taken a subway uptown. He admired on Fifty Seventh Street tall, folio-carrying women he assumed to be models. One crossed Seventh Avenue in front of him, as nimble on her high heels as a dancer, and the sidewalk crowd parted in admiration.

He studied paintings by Velasquez, Rubens and Rembrandt while draining several foolishly small glasses of wine. The sleek of the city glided around him. The woman in the blue dress stood alone, head cocked in front of a Cezanne. She settled on one muscled leg, rocked to the other. Her wheat field hair tumbled. A hand snaked, absent-minded, to smooth an errant tress.

Scott stepped behind her, exhibition catalog in hand. As yet he could not see her face. "Says here Cezanne had the courage to stop before he killed a picture with too many brushstrokes," he said.

She nodded, as if this explained all.

"Are you alone?" he asked.

"I was." She turned toward him: big, farm-girl blue eyes, wide, pretty face. She smiled and he saw a shadowed crevice between her two front teeth.

"Where did you get that drink?" she asked.

"Over by the door. Want one?"

"Please."

Scott pushed through the crowd to fetch her wine and hurried back. The gap between her teeth was still there. Already it possessed his imagination.

"I'm Brittany VanHorn."

"I'm Scott Lehmann."

They strolled together. Scott liked landscapes by Lorrain and Guardi. She exclaimed over Velaquez. The show spanned two crowded floors and even the stairs between teemed with people.

Brittany lived nearby, she said, and worked as a paralegal. "My boss wanted me to stay late tonight. He's a young man, quite good looking.

I told him, 'No, I must see this show.' I told him one of the older partners got me a ticket."

"That did it, then?"

"What?"

"The involvement of the older partner: so then your boss let you come to the art show?"

"My boss is married. Are you married?" She ignored his question and asked one of her own.

"No. Did you think I was?"

"So often the really attractive men are married. My tennis instructor is married. He wants me to go shopping with him so I can help him pick a racquet. I don't think that's such a good idea."

"Go with him," Scott said. He just wants to be helpful."

"What if I am attracted to him?"

"Piffle. You risk that thirty times a day."

They exited together into New York night and Scott suggested they stop for a drink and something to eat at a bistro on Madison Avenue. He ordered a Bourdeaux and held his glass against a candle. "See that smoldering red. Colors tell us things. I like my Scotch as smoky as old saddle leather."

"I like the smoldering green of one-hundred dollar bills."

Scott laughed. "To summer," he said, and they clinked glasses.

"You really think I should go with him?"

"Who?"

"My tennis instructor."

"I do." Scott said. He saw that it perplexed her that he resisted jealousy and this interested him. He enjoyed complexity. She hummed, a tune he did not recognize, and he felt the hum of the city. Had he met Brittany VanHorn back in his dusty little town he might have proposed to her already. Here, he thought, their mutual exploration of terrain, the tactics, the positioning, only began.

"So you are a stockbroker. Do you want to go into management someday?"

"No, I like what I do," Scott said. "They give me a desk and a telephone and leave me alone."

"You should meet my brother, he's a genius with computers. You think he should be happy, with all his skills, but he is not because he hates competition. I tell him that is the way business is, but he holds to what he calls his ideals, he does not see the necessity of struggle. I fought his fights for him when he was little."

"And now you remind him of that?"

"I do tease him about it, yes." Brittany laughed, and Scott glimpsed the gap, felt its musty pull. She's heartless, but she's forthright, he thought.

They strolled along a row of townhouses toward her apartment on East Sixty-First Street. Couples passed, talking softly. Trees looked waxed in the streetlights. It was one of those soft Manhattan blocks of trees and lights and brownstones that make you think you want to live forever.

Brittany invited Scott up and he watched the play of her legs as they climbed two flights of stairs. She flung open a window over the street. Want some Scotch?"

"A small one, please, after all that wine." He saw a kitchen, a bedroom, a few books above a couch.

She handed him a teak-colored drink. "Got any hot tips?" she asked, and laughed. "Do people really ask stockbrokers that?"

"More than you would think." Scott gazed down at the East Sixty- First Street. "I like your neighborhood."

"There's a gorgeous man down the hall who lives with a woman friend, but weekends he goes to the Hamptons and leaves her behind. That's pretty bold, don't you think?"

"Very bold." Did she lack confidence? he began to wonder. That might seem surprising, considering her multiple assets, but look at actors, look at politicians.

Scott kissed her and touched with his tongue that dark gap between her teeth. Something flashed in her eyes. Triumph? She pulled away. She began a story about a man she had met in a restaurant who continued to call and ask her out.

"Brittany, you don't have to prove you're desirable, I can see that for myself." He moved to kiss her again, but she dodged away. He saw her calculating wins and losses. Maybe they were not so different after all.

"There you stand," he said. "It's hard not to touch."

"I don't feel like romance right now."

He asked for her telephone number and she wrote it for him. Leave now, Scott told himself. As if realizing his intent, suddenly passionate, Brittany plunged her mouth to his.

"Ah." He backed her toward the couch.

"No." The victory look flashed again. Scott descended the stairs. Next time,he thought, he would feign indifference. Yawn. Eat a peanut.

One of the city's weary slumped against the wall in the subway station. A young man, a student probably, leaned over the derelict. "Promise me you will stop drinking," the young man said. "Promise."

"I promise," the old man said.

The student left. Scott gave the old guy a dollar. He had exhorted derelicts too when he first arrived in the city. He bought them meals, fancied that he changed their lives. Even now, though he knew better, he still experienced, in the midst of the city's wreckage, moments of freshness and wonder.

He flirted in the subway with an Hispanic girl across the aisle. She would be disappointed if he did not, he thought.

CHAPTER 7

"Blip, blip, blip, UPI, UPI, UPI," Art Levin did his sportscaster imitation. "They say you've lost a step, Lash Storm. They say the years and the pounding have torn at your being. They say the big fellow has seen his greatest seasons. What do you say to that, Lash Storm?"

"I say, 'Bosh,' Lamont Gramercy Cranston."

"Remember our summer house meeting in May? Remember the hordes of chicks we thought we'd meet?"

"July and August remain," Scott Lehmann said.

He came to work as usual this morning. He flicked on his terminal and watched numbers gleam to life. He checked the prices of gold and oil and what London did and how stock futures traded. He listened on a loudspeaker to his firms' analysts tout stocks they followed. Now he and Art Levin sat in the sun on the steps of the Federal Building across Wall Street from the New York Stock Exchange watching the women of the financial district promenade on their lunch hour.

"I thought I nailed a landlord this week," Art said. "Holes in the ceiling, holes in the walls, six warnings already. I sent it up to legal but my supervisor kicked it back. 'Do we really want to do this? We don't want to lose the rooms.' He and the landlord probably speculate together on East Hampton real estate."

"You can't go over your supervisor's head?"

"Not and keep my job." Art took a last bite of a hotdog he had purchased from a street vendor. He squinted at hard truths. "The landlords claim they rehabilitate, but we know they don't. We give them money anyway. The builders cheat on materials; we know they do. We give them money. I've had it with housing, Storm."

"You're inside the citadel, Lamont. Cleanse from within."

"It's too late for that. I'm living in sludge. When you get up in the morning and dread going to work, you know it's time for a change."

"What kind of change?"

"I'm twenty-nine years old, Storm. I've never lived anyplace but New York City. I've never lived more than ten miles from my parents. I'm twenty-nine and I've never lived away from home."

"You rent your own apartment. You are away."

"I'm not. I'm not away. My parents expect me for Sunday dinner. I could be a lawyer. I could bring pollution and class action suits. I could teach at a university. You know where I see myself? I see myself a professor at the University of Oregon."

"Eugene, Oregon? Oregon, Oregon?"

"That's it."

"Have you ever been there?"

"No, but I can picture it. Mountains. Big trees."

"That's a far step, Lamont. That's too far to take the subway home for dinner with mom and dad."

"Exactly. You jest, Storm, but inadvertently brush upon a positive. Law school: I'm just stroking the idea, you understand. Don't mention it next weekend at Davis Park, okay?"

Scott rode the elevator upstairs to his office. George Rogalski stared out his window at workmen enclosing another floor atop the south tower of the World Trade Center. Barry Kalish glanced up from a thicket of research reports. "All analysts went to Harvard," he said. On terminals all around yellow-green numbers raced restlessly on.

Scott intended to telephone Brittany VanHorn and propose dinner in Greenwich Village, but now he hesitated. That urge, that prickly urge, for the moment deserted him.

Barry's head rose above the partition between their desks. "They stopped trading in Rico Chemical."

Scott punched up RCO on his terminal. An icon indicated recent news, and he searched and found it; officials at Rico forecast second quarter earnings well above what the Street had expected. When the stock resumed trading, it would surely open higher.

Ingrid Henson had bought Rico for herself and the two ZaneCorp executives at prices under forty-five. Scott called her, told her about the new earnings forecast, and predicted the stock would resume trading several points higher.

"That's good," she said.

"I'll say." Scott had expected Ingrid to respond to the news with more excitement.

"See if you can sell Mr. Crosland's, Mr. Irvin's and my own shares at fifty-two." That would give them over seven dollars a share profit in less than two weeks.

Commissions, Scott thought. His spirits rekindled. "I enter the orders as we speak."

He called her back an hour later. The stock reopened at fifty-three and she and the others sold at that price. Now it traded at fifty-one.

Scott wanted to ask who at that charity ball advised Mr. Crosland to buy the stock, and why, but that breached etiquette, and besides it was sometimes better not to know. He should have bought the stock himself. He could have, justifiably, for his own firm's analyst had recommended it.

"That worked out well," Ingrid said.

"Yes, it's not a profit until you take it," Scott mouthed one of his brokerage bromides. He anticipated, with the commissions from these trades, one of his better days of the month.

George Rogalski wandered into view. "I don't believe it," he said. "Rico Chemical trades above fifty."

"Our analyst recommended it, you know." Scott, gleeful, snatched George's handkerchief from his pocket and pretended to blow his nose. "You secretly wanted me to do that, George."

"And you were perceptive enough to realize it," George said.

Office manager Walter Cappaletti strolled down the aisle. "You had some customers in Rico, right?"

"Some of the people at ZaneCorp and a few others," Scott said.

"Didn't buy any for yourself?"

"No, Walter, I missed out on this one."

"Rejoice," Walter said, "we have some eager lawyers in compliance and we don't want to excite their curiosity." He turned, as if to fling a discus, instead flung a smile at Monica Corbin.

Walter neared fifty, but only flecks of gray peppered his abundant hair. He had played baseball in college, still jogged on weekends. He had five kids and lived on Long Island. Office managers usually had lots of kids. George Rogalski said the more kids a man had, the more Tuttle, Osborn & Durkin had him.

Walter spoke to Monica and his hand rested on her shoulder. She shook her head, amused, and Walter winked at Scott, who recalled – a happy image – how at office parties their leader liked to dance with the women brokers and was always one of the last to leave.

Now, what was it he intended to do? Yes, call Brittany VanHorn, but Monica waved to catch his attention. "Jennifer Cohen on line three."

Jennifer Cohen? He hoisted his telephone.

"Hello, Scott, how are you today? Scott, I represent a nationally known brokerage firm that wants to staff its flagship office here in New York City with outstanding brokers. We offer an excellent package of benefits and we know of your past success. We consider you..."

"Let me save your time, I'm happy here." Scott frequently got these headhunter calls, as did many of the brokers in the office, and usually he signed off quickly. But this headhunter possessed a husky, interesting voice. "Call me again in a year if you like," he said.

"Please, all I ask is twenty minutes of your time to sit down and talk. I'm confident you will be happy to hear what I have to say. You're at the corner of Broadway and Wall, Croupers is a block away; why don't I meet you at Croupers at five-thirty."

Scott hesitated. As a salesman himself, he appreciated a good spiel. But, of more importance, he began to wonder how the possessor of this voice at the other end of the line might look in person. He had nothing planned after work, and he liked the name Jennifer. A third of the girls born in the metropolitan area in the late forties were probably named Jennifer. He had met three or four interesting Jennifers already at Davis Park; maybe she was one of these. "How will I recognize you?" he asked.

"I'll carry a yellow balloon," she said. "I'm kidding; I'm wearing a black skirt with a white blouse and I have dark hair and I'll sit near the door."

"Look for me in a gray suit and red tie."

"Are you tall?"

"Six-two."

"Sandy, tousled hair?"

He laughed. "What is this, anyway?"

"It's been a long day," Jennifer Cohen said.

CHAPTER 8

Scott Lehmann slung his coat over his shoulder and walked around the corner to Croupers.

"Scott?"

Jennifer Cohen sat on a bar stool with her legs crossed and she rose to shake hands. She wore shiny, flat-heeled black patent shoes, a dark skirt and a white blouse. She had brown eyes and a tan, stood about five-feet-seven, and her black hair riffed across her forehead and descended behind to an inch above her collar. She moved athletically and without self-consciousness. "Did you have a busy day?" she asked.

"I did," he said. "What about you?" He searched, almost hopefully, for a flaw in her appearance, but could not find one.

"I met with several brokers. And now you're here."

"Something alcoholic?" He saw that she nursed a Perrier.

"No thanks. Shall we take a table?"

They still stood along the bar. Scott considered: a table meant twenty, thirty minutes at least. "Let's do," he said.

He ordered a Bloody Mary. "On me," Jennifer immediately said.

"No, I'll get it." Scott contemplated her tan. "The Hamptons," he guessed.

"Close. I'm in a house in Amagansett." This was beyond the Hamptons, further out toward the eastern end of Long Island.

"I'm at Davis Park on Fire Island."

"I considered Fire Island, I almost joined a house. I guess it's the ferry ride that put me off."

"It lends a feeling of adventure," Scott said. "Everything seems possible, crossing Great South Bay."

"Well." She looked at him, Scott thought, as if he had just said something interesting. "How long are you in the brokerage business?"

"Three years."

"Production? Do you mind me asking?"

"Not at all. My goal is four hundred this year." He exaggerated, but not much, because she probably already knew his numbers. Four-hundred thousand dollars in annual commissions, though not spectacular, ranked high at that time for a third-year man.

"I could get you a deal."

"If I wanted a change, I could get myself a deal."

"Not this good."

Scott rubbed his chin. "Who's your client?"

"Actually, I'm working a startup but I'm thinking now that's not for you. I'm thinking I can get you bigger bucks from an established house. Maybe a bonus up front, a higher payout on commissions, a title. Would you like that?"

"A title." Scott visualized "Vice President" placards on his door and his desk. But Jennifer said on the telephone that she staffed a "flagship office," now she pushed a startup. She's creating, he thought, and if my numbers check out she'll shop me around.

"I'm happy where I am," he said.

"Did you decide that before you came?"

"I wanted to hear what you had to say. I am wondering what happened to that 'flagship office' you mentioned on the telephone."

"It's there, they're there; I can match you up just about anywhere if you're interested."

"Let me think about it," Scott said. He did not want to just say no.

"Good." She downed the last of her Perrier and rose as if to go. "I'll contact you again."

"Don't hurry; I'm curious about your business." Scott waved for the waitress. "How many others did you meet this afternoon?"

Jennifer sat back down. "You're the fourth and final." The waitress came, and she ordered a vodka and tonic.

"Tell me," Scott said, "did you grow up in the city?"

Jennifer glanced outside, where on this July afternoon the temperature registered in the nineties. Her black hair riffed across her head, stirred and settled. "I grew up in Great Neck on Long Island and graduated from Cornell in business."

"I'm from Illinois and I majored in history in college. I took my minor in business and sold advertising for the *Minneapolis Tribune*. Lunchtime in the Twin Cities I liked to watch the moving tape at a brokerage office down the street. One day it occurred to me, 'Hey, you enjoy this so much, why don't you try it as a career?' I applied to several brokerage firms. Here I am. How did you become a headhunter?"

"I started in resort management at Cornell and worked my freshman summer at my uncle's hotel in Miami beach. I didn't like it, so my sophomore year I switched my major to business."

"What didn't you like?"

"I didn't like the people. I didn't like working for my uncle. I didn't like the heat."

"You like stockbrokers better?"

"Look around," Jennifer said. "I'm in New York."

Scott ordered another Bloody Mary. "I took courses in philosophy," he said. "I liked Teilhard de Chardin comparing mankind to a giant brain."

"Thus anticipating computers," Jennifer said, "but philosophy doesn't explain sunburns or buying groceries."

"What weekends do you go to Amagansett?"

"I go every other. This coming weekend's mine."

"We're on the same schedule," Scott said. "How about that?"

She blew upward on her hair.

"Last summer I guested in a house at Amagansett and we went to a party," Scott said. "I remember candles in driveways and strange- colored drinks."

"That was probably our house."

"Big place? Swimming pool?"

"No pool, we're near the ocean. I like to get up early and walk the beach because it's the only time out there I can be alone."

"I'm that way too," Scott said. He nudged his chair closer. "Do you like to hike?"

"Hike?"

"Yes," he said, "in the woods."

"Aren't there bugs?"

"There's hiking and there's hiking. There's strolling around pretty lakes and there's mud and guts backpacking."

"I've never done any mud and guts backpacking," Jennifer said. "I like tennis, I like to swim. I live next to Lincoln Center, so that's convenient for the arts."

"One of my clients invited me to the Hermitage art exhibit last week," Scott said. "You didn't make that, by any chance?"

"No, I read about it after. You said you sold advertising. What was that like?"

"They paid us commissions according to how much we sold, so it wasn't so different from what I do now. But it was dusty dry compared to the moving, translucent numbers."

She smiled. "'The moving, translucent numbers;' I can use that in my recruiting."

"Do you see what's happening here? We're communicating. How about dinner tonight?"

"I'm sorry, I made plans," Jennifer said, "but let's swap business cards."

The heat hit like a hammer outside. "Share a cab," Scott suggested.

"Where do you live?" she asked.

"I'm on West Twentieth. I can walk from Sixth Avenue." He flagged a taxi, they hopped in. Jennifer crossed her legs and glanced at her watch.

"Maybe next week we could do something in the city together," Scott said.

"Call me."

"I will."

❖   ❖   ❖

.

CHAPTER 9

A kid in a Mets cap approached as if he waited just for them. "Good seats, mister. Take 'em at cost."

The scalper reduced his price because in minutes the game began. Scott Lehmann examined the tickets and bought two. The kid gave him change from a thick wad of bills and Scott saw he still held other tickets to sell. "What happens if you don't move them all?" he asked.

"Never happen," the kid said.

They pushed through a turnstile. "Another twenty minutes, he'll offer them below cost," Jennifer Cohen said.

Scott had called her Wednesday to suggest this Friday night baseball game, reasoning that if she said no he could rationalize it as too last minute, but if she said yes he could interpret that as encouragement. They rode the subway out from Grand Central. He didn't need to impress her financially, he thought, because she probably had checked him out and knew she dated a rising star.

Jennifer, racy in a short skirt, striped jersey and flat, shiny shoes, strode ahead of him up a concrete ramp in Shea Stadium.

A breeze idled through the open sides of the structure and Scott noted patterned rows of parked cars below. A noise grew, the sound of many people, and they walked out into an explosion of light. An usher pointed. Their seats looked directly down on home plate.

The Mets, as home team, ran out on the grass. Ping, ping, ping; a baseball darted around the infield as if on a string. It had amazed Scott as a boy, watching the Chicago Cubs in Wrigley Field, when the infielders cocked their arms and effortlessly rifled these bullets – ping, ping, ping. That impressed him even more than the hitting.

He smelled beer and peanuts and dusty summer. The playing field below them glowed in arc lights, a meadow of iridescent green.

"Been here before?" Scott asked.

"Never," Jennifer said.

"Yankee Stadium?"

"No. This is my first baseball game."

"If I had suggested a parachute jump..." He smiled, touched her arm.

The crowd rose for the national anthem. Scott thought of all the times in high school and college he had stood on football fields and basketball courts, a player himself, listening to the anthem, waiting for another game to begin. He had believed as a boy that his country could do no wrong.

"Who are those people out there?"

"That's the bullpens, the extra pitchers and catchers."

"This is interesting. I'm enjoying this."

The game began. Every soft blooper the Mets hit seemed to fall in, while every line-drive the Phillies smote whistled directly at someone. Thus the score mounted in favor of the home team and the tension of the game ebbed away. "Beer. Popcorn." Hawkers prowled the aisles. Scott bought a beer. Summer twilight faded and the lights of Queens blinked beyond the stadium.

Young men clapped each other on the shoulders and sloshed beer and waved fingers as the score mounted. "We're number one," they chanted. "We're number one!"

"'We're number one.' What the hell do they have to do with it, anyway," Scott said.

Jennifer studied him as if she stumbled upon some new, interesting facet of character. "Do you bring your customers to games?"

"No. Do you take yours to dinner, to Broadway plays?"

"Rarely."

"There might be times when that could be to your advantage," Scott said. He liked it that she forced him to explain himself. "What I mean," he continued, "is that I never got in the habit of entertaining customers, so I guess they don't expect it. I do take someone to lunch now and then."

"You do have an expense account?"

"Well, sparingly."

"Let your company pay," Jennifer said. "Take advantage." On the field below the Mets tallied another run. Jennifer gazed beyond, toward the eastern sky. "Here comes the moon," she said.

Scott stared across the flatness of Long Island spotted with the shapes of buildings and remembered his little town in Illinois, where the prairie stretched away as level and uninterrupted as the ocean. There the moon rose huge and liquid. Trees floated like mirages across the fields of summer.

"Great Neck's over there." Jennifer pointed a little to the right of centerfield.

"Illinois." Scott glanced to his left. He turned and looked almost directly behind him. "The Adirondacks."

They left after the eighth inning to get ahead of the crowd and Jennifer trotted beside him on her shiny shoes. She turned to face him on the subway platform, breathing briskly, breasts moistly outlined beneath her blouse. "What are you, Baptist or something?"

"Because I walk fast, because I don't entertain my customers?"

"I'm speaking in general terms here."

"My parents considered themselves Lutheran."

"Lutheran. Doesn't that involve dank columns, people chanting?"

"I haven't been to church in several years but I can tell you that no one chanted. It is intense, though; there's a hard edge of excitement."

"Oh, I'm sure," Jennifer said. The subway arrived, absorbed them, clattered past apartment buildings and slid underground. Scott darted glances at people across the aisle. Three years in the city, he thought, and still a voyeur.

"Who do you usually go out with?" he asked.

"Who do I date?"

"Yes. Inside the faith or out?"

"Mostly inside, I suppose," Jennifer said.

"So why did you go out with me?"

"What, you're hoping for praise?"

"You saw through me," Scott said.

"I was curious, if you want to know."

"That's right, you'd never seen a Mets game."

"Oh sure, I wanted to see somebody steal second. Why did you ask me? You like Jewish women?"

"I'm practicing. That's all I meet at Davis Park."

"You caught me at the right time," Jennifer said. "Right now I'm between men."

"Not for long, one wagers."

"'One wagers?' I don't believe you said that."

They caught a cab outside Grand Central. Jennifer gave an address and they rode to a big building on Broadway near Lincoln Center. "Want to come up?" she asked.

Scott nodded yes. "Evening, Miss Cohen," the doorman said. She punched floor number ten in the elevator.

"Just for a little while, my sister visits early tomorrow. She's married and lives in Bronxville. She's a shopping mall person, and she likes to start early."

Jennifer's apartment appeared cluttered with books and records and, ponderous in her living room, a piano nudged a wall. A painting above her couch depicted a river and misty, shadowy buildings. Scott peered at the title beneath; it was a print of Monet's *Houses of Parliament*. "You play the piano?" he asked.

"Yes. Do you?"

"No. I play the guitar a little."

"Come out here." She opened a door to a terrace and Scott walked out, leaned on an iron railing and gazed down at Central Park.

"Nice," he said.

"I'm going to make tea. Do you want some?"

"Please, with honey and milk."

"I take mine with honey too."

"Great minds. I also take vitamins."

"That's smart," Jennifer said. "I do too."

Scott eyed her legs, her frisky waist. She did look healthy. "For breakfast," he said, "I fill a bowl with wheat germ, slice a banana on top and pour in whole milk."

"Tell me what you do for lunch."

"I usually buy a cup of tea and an apple raisin muffin and if the weather's nice I sit on the steps of the Federal Building and watch the people walk by."

"Myself, I like tuna sandwiches and apple juice, and there's a patio outside our building where I sit when I'm not chasing down brokers."

"Where is your building."

"Park Avenue in the Fifties."

"That's a pleasant area. May I?" Scott noticed a photo album, and while Jennifer made tea he opened it to pictures of two little girls and a young couple, the woman long-haired, big-breasted, the man jaunty, tilting toward heavy. The house behind looked new, no shrubs, no trees on the lawn.

Jennifer returned with tea and peered over his shoulder. "Where is this, the streets of Laredo?" Scott asked.

"Levittown. We moved from there to Great Neck. Dad's a doctor; internal medicine. See, he frowns in this picture, he's thinking 'younger woman.' He and my mother divorced. She's still in Great Neck. He lives in Connecticut and practices in Manhattan."

"You're close to both?"

"We talk."

Scott turned pages, years passed, her mother gained weight. Jennifer sat on the couch beside him. "You?" she asked.

"My parents divorced about ten years ago and neither remarried. They live six blocks apart in the same little town." He turned a page in her photo album. "Here's you when, eighth grade? Wow! You developed early."

"Check out my my sister." Jennifer flipped another page.

"Oh my. And what's this! Look at you!"

"My first bikini. Mother didn't like it. We argued a lot around the dinner table after dad left, my mother, my sister and me. Sometimes I watched television shows about polite WASP families and thought how nice it would be to grow up like that."

"You see?" Scott said. "I thought people needed to be ethnic, to yell at each other, to achieve family warmth."

"I still think it's the Protestants who live sober, sensible lives."

"Not so," Scott said. "Those vagrants you see sleeping on grates; they're our guys. The public shelters of America teem with Methodists and Presbyterians." He turned another page in the album. "Hallelujah. Where's this?"

"It's my father's new house on the Connecticut shore."

"The woman? I can't see her very well."

"His second wife."

"She's young?"

"She was. Really, I do have to get up early."

"Have you ever visited Davis Park? No? Why don't you come out next weekend as my guest."

"This coming weekend?"

"Yes."

"What are the sleeping arrangements?"

"Same room, different beds."

"You assume I'm a sure thing?"

"No, no," Scott backtracked. "There's four other regulars besides me, so it's not overcrowded. I like to spend most of my day on the beach, as does virtually everyone, but that's optional and of course depends on the weather. It can get dismal when it rains. Unlike Amagansett, there's only one place to go at night, the Casino, but then there are private parties."

"You changed your mind?" Jennifer asked. "Now you're trying to talk me out of it?"

"I present the picture in full, to avoid disappointment."

"Can we wait for a weather forecast and then decide?"

"We can do that." Scott rose, prepared to depart before she changed her mind. Jennifer walked him to the door. Should he kiss her? He leaned, their lips touched. She did not pull away. Now he would hope for good weather this weekend.

CHAPTER 10

"Barry, where did you work summers when you were in college?" Monica Corbin asked.

'Why do you want to know?"

"I'm writing a book," Monica said. She sat on her desk, swinging her red high heels.

"Come on, Barry, tell her," Scott Lehmann said.

"I worked as a counselor at a summer camp in Massachusetts."

"You did? Why didn't you tell me before? I went to Bennington and worked three summers in Vermont. We share a New England connection."

"That's exciting," Barry said.

"Barry, tell her what you used to do up at Goose Pond," Scott said.

"I hooked a plastic bottle over the sun visor of my car and filled it with vodka and ran a tube down so I could drink as I drove around."

"That's good, isn't it?" Scott said.

"Sensational," Monica said.

"Tell her about the stewardess," Scott said. According to Barry, a Danish airline stewardess accidentally poured a martini into his lap at a party, and to make up for it she invited him to her hotel room.

"You tell her," Barry said. His telephone rang and he snatched it up. He frowned. "Damn you, Golden Falcon, don't tie up my line!"

Monica picked up. "Hello, Bruce." It was not yet nine in the morning and already Bruce Stanton called from his end of the office. Monica lowered her voice and Scott saw her smile.

The squawk box crackled to life and Walter Cappaletti's voice announced a meeting. Brokers disliked meetings; bitch, bitch, grumble, grumble, they filed into rows of seats in a room set aside for such events. Latecomers stood at the rear.

"What's the best investment any of us made in the last ten years?" Walter swept them with his gaze. "That's right; not stocks, not bonds; the best investment any of us made was real estate. The best investment we made was buying our homes." He paused and glared at them. "And that's how we will present RMF Properties."

These real estate packages came along about twice a year. The people who sponsored them offered big commissions both to individual brokers and to their brokerage firms. But Scott had never owned a home and he daydreamed as Walter droned on... "Sorry, Jennifer, there's only one bed." "Oh that's okay, if you don't mind that I forgot my nightie..."

"...shopping malls. Garden apartments. Eight per cent annual payout..." Scott wondered how high Walter Cappaletti aimed, because no one with an Italian name had ever headed Tuttle, Osborn & Durkin. Irish Catholics prevailed and they, like managements everywhere, tended to elevate their own.

But Walter was different, he walked with an angel on his shoulder.

He charmed his superiors at martini lunches, he was accessible, his underlings liked him. Scott knew of office managers as opaque as shower doors. Walter already made a quarter million a year and Scott wondered if he possessed the fire in his belly. Why should he want the aggravation of new responsibilities? Why spend his weekends playing golf with the same twelve red-faced men?

"...really do a job on this one. Top guy or gal I'm buying lunch. Surely you've all got clients on your books you want to call..."

The meeting ended. George Rogalski, eternally eager in his 1950s crewcut, toted a pile of RMF prospectuses back to his office. Scott stuck his head in. "Going to push this one?" he asked.

"I think it has some interesting aspects." George sat amid his stack of prospectuses all that afternoon, seemingly unaware of the summer sun in its cloudless sky, hunched over his telephone.

Scott bought a cup of tea and an apple raisin muffin and joined Brent Hall at noon on the steps of the Federal Building.

"You ready?" Brent asked.

"I'm ready." They would meet after work at the outdoor basketball court at West Fourth and Bleecker, where guys came from all over the city to compete and passersby clung to the wire fence to watch. The Leroy Street gym attracted good players. The playground at West Fourth and Bleecker represented the Big Time.

Two young women strolled by on the sidewalk in front of the Federal Building, coltish, brightly dressed. Scott followed them with his eyes. "Did you call the speech therapist?" he asked.

"We talked," Brent said. "She said she likes to go out of town on weekends and as you know I don't own a car. I gave as a reason that in the West Village it is difficult to park. I could rent, of course. I told her that. I told her I do know how to drive."

"You don't need a car to take her to an off Broadway play."

"Give me time. I call her again now, she thinks, 'Mother of Mary, the redneck again.'"

"Does she realize you edit textbooks? Does she realize the importance of what you do?"

Brent considered. "I think she does."

"Call her," Scott said. "What's the worst that could happen?"

"The world could be plunged into eternal darkness."

"A headhunter called and tried to recruit me for another firm. Her name is Jennifer Cohen and I took her to a Mets game."

"That's good. She's a sports fan."

"Incipient sports fan. She lives on Central Park West and she said it was her first baseball game. She's coming to Davis Park this weekend as my guest."

"Whoa! So soon? This will be a good test," Brent said.

"I know. I wondered if I was moving too fast."

"What's the worst that could happen?" Brent asked.

"She drowns. Both of us drown." Scott returned to his office and again checked the weekend weather forecast.

He rode the subway home, changed, and caught another subway back down to West Fourth Street and Sixth Avenue. Greenwich Village baked in the sun. An aging movie theater exhaled dust, restaurants smelled of linguine. Scott bounced his basketball across Sixth Avenue and looked for Brent.

Nearby, in a pleasant, little park under dusty trees, ragged men passed a bottle in a paper bag. Brent walked down the street in shorts, t-shirt and sneakers and he and Scott approached the site of today's action. Six or seven black guys shot baskets at one end of a concrete basketball court surrounded by a high wire fence. One sprang and effortlessly stuffed a shot. He eyed the newcomers. "Want to go?"

Scott nodded. This is what he came for. You want serious basketball in the city, you compete with the blacks.

They played full court, four on four, and onlookers collected along the wire fence. Scott averaged twenty-nine points a game in Minneapolis the winter after he graduated from college, playing independent ball against doughy white guys like himself. But could he hold his own here on the mean streets? He always wondered when he took to the asphalt at West Fourth and Sixth Avenue.

He felt slow and embarrassed his first few times up and down the court and blacks on the opposing team slapped hands, exchanged looks. Then Brent banked an illogical shot from the side. He hit another. Scott nailed a jumper. He began to feel the flow.

The jive talk ended, the game began. Back and forth they surged, back and forth. Scott forgot the moving yellow-green numbers and his monthly sales goals. Time slowed.

They played another game, another, while above the city wispy clouds cooled from pink to purple and below a group of men played basketball until it grew too dark to see.

Scott, Brent and the youngest of the black guys leaned on the wire fence afterward, reluctant to leave.

"I ain't that big," the kid said. "I see baseball as my chance to make it to the big leagues. I like shortstop, but I expect they'll put me in the pasture."

"That's right, outfield's where you want your good hitters," Brent said. Behind them men who never made it to the big leagues tipped wine bottles beneath the trees.

Scott bounced his basketball along the sidewalk, enjoying the pebbled feel on his fingers, and he and Brent walked up West Fourth toward Seventh Avenue. "I called the speech therapist," Brent said. "I take her to a folk music concert Friday."

"What's her name?"

"Ruth Challender. Challender as in challenge." He turned off as usual at West Eleventh and Scott continued on toward his apartment on West Twentieth. He glanced up at the Empire State Building and the colored lights that illuminate the top suddenly flared on. An omen, Scott thought. You had to look at just the right moment to see that.

But what kind of omen? He and Jennifer Cohen hardly knew each other, and he invited her to share a weekend on an island where he himself still felt a newcomer. Scott Lehmann bounced his basketball homeward and considered his options.

Ask her questions, he told himself. Listen to the answers.

CHAPTER 11

"Did you really have a specific firm in mind when you called that day to recruit me?" Scott Lehmann wore his seersucker business suit and spread his legs for balance in the bar car Friday afternoon on the way to Patchogue. His weekend with Jennifer Cohen began.

"Yes and no. I like to get to know my prospects, to see them in action." Jennifer had changed at home to Capri pants, a striped t-shirt and sandals. Scott noticed their reflection in a window, he in suit and tie, she earth-mother casual. It appeared they belonged to different tribes.

"It might be deceiving to observe me in action," Scott said. "I try to make it look effortless, like a star center fielder." She smiled, but it struck Scott, listening to himself, that ever since meeting Jennifer at Penn Station he groped for his natural, fluid flow.

"Look effortless for your sales assistant," she said. "For management, look like you're working hard."

The train jerked, their cups sloshed. Scott steadied himself. "Happily, stock brokering is tangible," he said. "You add your commissions at the end of the day. There it is."

"It's true, it's easy to keep score. We do that in my business too. I recruited a big hitter for Livingston, Sheldon today."

"That's a nice glow, when you sit down and realize you've had a good day," Scott said. They shared a camaraderie, he thought, since headhunter Jennifer worked in a way as a salesperson too. "How big a hitter is he?"

"SHE's a six-hundred thousand dollar producer."

Their eyes met. Scott smiled. "How long in the business?" he asked.

"Four years."

"Pretty good."

"It's scandalous the money some of you make," Jennifer said. "I may become a stockbroker myself."

An image flashed for Scott, Jennifer in her shiny shoes, tapping a pencil against her teeth, pitching a hot stock to a client. He felt himself begin to relax. "You already know the key words," he said.

She scrunched her brow. "What do you say to a customer when you want him to sell?"

"If the stock's down, I say, 'Bob, let your profits run but cut your losses. Let's get rid of this dog.' If the stock's up, I say, 'You'll never go broke taking profits, Morton.'"

"What happened to letting your profits run?"

"The same adage doesn't apply in every situation."

"As long as you keep your adages straight."

Scott chuckled and rocked with the jolting train. "If it's a good market, I say, 'A rising tide lifts all boats.' If it's a bad market, I say, 'When the paddy wagon comes, they take the good girls along with the bad.'"

Jennifer laughed. "If I opened an account, what would you say to me?"

"'Jennifer, if you do what you're told, your pockets will be filled with silver and gold.'"

"Well. That would instill confidence."

Barry likes, 'Bulls make money. Bears make money. Pigs get left out in the cold.' George says, 'The trend is your friend.'"

"Slower," Jennifer joked. "I'm trying to remember all this."

Scott waved his drink. "Never eat at a place called Mom's. Never buy a noon-hour rally."

"Why not a noon-hour rally? Lighter volume, you mean? Not trustworthy because some of the players are away from their desks?"

"Both," Scott said. "Right on both counts."

Jennifer's earrings swung, bright balls at the ends of golden chains. Scott saw other men study her up and down. "You look especially good today," he said.

"Maybe I'm wearing my golden haze."

"'Golden haze?'"

"It's from Virginia Woolf's *To The Lighthouse*. When the woman feels irresistible, she says she's wearing her golden haze."

"I like that." Scott sipped his drink. The train rocked, their thighs touched.

They shared a taxi from the railroad station to the ferry with two young women and Scott sat in front with the driver and compared the streets of Patchogue to an enchanted village.

"Peopled with elves," Jennifer got into the spirit of the thing. The two young women studied their knees and absolutely refused to smile. They passed a brown cottage. "The gingerbread house," Scott tried again, determined to win the strangers over. One of them rolled her eyes.

He climbed with Jennifer to the top deck of the ferry. The breeze smelled of salt and sea and glowing airplane trails crisscrossed a sunset sky. "We charmed those two girls in the taxi," Scott said. "I think they only feigned indifference."

"Tell me about the people in your house."

Scott began with their jobs and where they lived in the city.

"Larry's the organizer?"

"Right. Art's the rhymer." A pier extended, the ferry bumped home, they strode away on a wooden walk. Gaslights glowed in houses on stilts. The ocean boomed beyond the darkened dune.

"Lehmann got a date." Larry Silverman occupied his usual perch at the far end of the bar. Barbara Feldstein in thick sweater and jeans, clutched her guitar. Art Levin still wore his city suit and tie. Scott introduced Jennifer around.

"Pounds, phennings, foreign monies; seems to me you picked a honey," Art said.

"Electric clock, laser timer; at last I meet the master rhymer." Jennifer had prepared. Art beamed and puffed his pipe.

Scott led Jennifer downstairs. "Damn." Someone had occupied the room he expected. He shot back upstairs. "Who took the guest room?"

"Marlene brought a guest," Larry said.

"No fair. I thought I reserved."

"You know the rules. First come..."

Scott knew the rules. He and Jennifer now faced a college dorm situation, he to room with Larry and Art, she with Barbara. They retreated back downstairs and Scott hoisted Jennifer's overnight bag to an upper bunk.

"Summer houses," she said. "It happens."

"Drat." Scott had visualized intimacy, a natural progression of smiles and sex. He had counted on the Celebrity Suite.

"Bunks. Are you kidding? It would have been awkward under the best of circumstances," Jennifer said.

Why had he worried? She sounded an old hand at this. He eyed her Capri pants and striped t-shirt. "I'll shed this suit," he said.

"That's the spirit. I'll wait upstairs."

Scott changed and climbed to join the others. Barbara Feldstein spread breads and sandwich ingredients and three kinds of cheese across the counter. Larry opened bottles of red and white wines.

"Where's Marlene?" Scott asked after Marlene Miller.

"She's with her guy," Larry said. "We'll see them at the Casino."

Jennifer created sandwiches for her and Scott. They sat along the counter chewing. Art carried his plate to the sink, rinsed it and pulled out his pipe.

"Art, why do you smoke that pipe?" Barbara asked. "Do you really like it, or is it just another way to attract attention?"

Larry grinned, Jennifer looked surprised and Scott imagined a scene in a western movie, guns unholstered, the barroom suddenly still.

Art furrowed as if thinking, nodded benignly. "Barbara, Barbara, thy venom flows; ease thy fury, some kindness show."

Luck, Scott thought. He had prepared a rhyme of his own while changing downstairs. "Chance arrival, happenstance, I think it's time to go and dance."

"Yes, and Barbara, you come with us," house organizer Larry said.

"She won't," Art said.

"I will," Barbara said.

"This is Big," Art said. "Give me a minute to change." He dashed below. The others swept away dishes and idled on the deck. It was a warm summer night. Waves slapped in beyond the dune. Art burst forth bare chested in his leather vest, Barbara followed in slacks and a blouse instead of bulky sweater. Jennifer took Scott's arm and the five of them thumped away on a wooden walk.

They climbed the stairs to the Casino. The place shook with noise. Scott ordered gin and tonics and hid them behind the jukebox while he and Jennifer danced. Marlene Miller appeared, sewn into white shorts so tight they creviced into the crease of her behind. She introduced her companion, a tanned man in a blue denim shirt, Arnold Saperstein, corporate attorney.

"We've met," Jennifer said. She and Arnold remembered each other from parties the summer before in East Hampton.

"Arnold's in the tennis invitational tomorrow at Ocean Beach," Marlene said.

Jennifer looked interested. Scott cast about for a way to change the subject. Art Levin prospected a blonde down the bar. Barbara stood near the door, talking with someone she knew.

Arnold asked Jennifer to dance, so Scott danced with Marlene. "Come with us to the tennis tournament tomorrow," she said. "We're taking a sand taxi down. Arnold's got a good chance to win."

Scott imagined he and Jennifer trapped on hard seats in wooden stands, rising dutifully to applaud when Arnold slashed another ace. "I kind of have my heart set on sun and sea," he said.

"Ask Jennifer," Marlene said. "Take a vote."

Scott looked for Jennifer and led her out on the balcony. "I don't want to spend tomorrow watching tennis." he said.

"Fine. I was just being polite."

"Good." Scott cast an experienced eye toward the sea. "Imagine a wall of ice higher than the Empire State Building sliding toward us from the north," he said. "That's what happened. The last great ice sheet scraped south from Canada fifteen thousand years ago and stopped not far from here."

"I know it left a hill down the middle of Long Island," Jennifer said. "I know that today people build houses on it. I remember all this stuff from junior high."

"The terminal moraine. We had one in Illinois."

"We're smart. Jennifer said. "We know things."

"Picture the moment the ice pauses at its exact southern limit. It starts to melt. Day one it retreats an inch..."

Jennifer rolled her eyes. "I like that song that's playing now. Let's go back inside."

Larry Silverman asked her to dance the moment she appeared in the door. "Where's Barbara?" Scott asked Art Levin.

"She said she was going back to the house."

"Did she dance with anybody?"

"Are you kidding?"

"Come on Lamont. Get involved. Let's try and get her to the Sixish tomorrow."

It was crowded, hot. Scott danced with Jennifer. She leaned in tight, and he suggested a walk on the beach. Clouds sailed above them toward Portugal, and a moon skipped between the cracks.

"Four of us, me, my friend and our dates, drove all the way to Lake Michigan after our high school prom in Illinois," Scott said. "We parked, we looked at the water, we turned around, we drove back."

"I went to my senior prom with a basketball player named Danny McMahon. He was left handed. My father couldn't stand him."

"Because he was left handed?"

"He wasn't Jewish, for one thing." They strolled on wet, hard sand.

"Did you ever almost marry?" Scott asked.

"Larry Goldblum at Cornell. He was gorgeous. If you saw him on the street, you'd think, 'That's a handsome man.'"

"What happened?"

"I drifted. That's my pattern."

Scott kissed her. She opened her mouth and her arms circled his neck. He lifted, gripping her tightly, roughly, and he felt her gasp and respond. Interesting. He must remember that.

They walked a mile or more, sat on upturned rowboat and talked and turned back. Scott led her over the dune toward their house. Gas lights flickered. Barbara Feldstein's guitar stood propped in a corner. "Looks like the others have gone to bed," he said.

"Maybe we should too."

"I could get a blanket. We could go back to the beach."

"Not yet. Let's save it, my friend."

Downstairs, turning in his bunk, Scott heard muffled sounds from the room that Marlene and Arnold shared. That should have been him and Jennifer. He pulled a pillow over his head.

In the morning Arnold lolled on the deck in gleaming tennis whites, his teeth flashing in summer sun. "Coming with us?" Marlene asked. She had telephoned for a dunes taxi.

Larry, Art and Barbara muttered excuses. "Maybe we'll come later."

Scott walked Jennifer to the beach. A silent ship slid along the curve of the ocean. Jennifer's swimsuit angled high at the hips and swooped tightly between her legs. He spread their beach blanket. "How about a jog along the sand?"

"Do you run in the city?" Jennifer asked.

"Sometimes in Central Park," he said. "What about you?"

"I use those running machines in the gym."

"Let's go," he said. "You'll thank me."

They ran along the water's edge, perspiring in the morning sun.

Jennifer rose high on her toes and Scott felt like a bulky animal beside her. They turned after about thirty minutes, trotted back, swam in the ocean and flopped in the sun.

"Huzza, huzza, hip, hip hooray; rise up, Storm, it's time to play." Art Levin loped toward them in his football jersey. Scott jumped to his feet and he, Art and Larry competed in touch football against the men from another house.

Jennifer in sunglasses watched. Grumbling strangers lobbed the football back after errant, gritty throws. Barbara Feldstein, nose coated in white, lay cloistered in cloth reading one of the novels she periodically assigned to her students. Jennifer conversed with a couple she knew.

Football game ended, Scott ran with her again into the ocean, the Atlantic Ocean chilly even in July. They lay in the sun and he touched little golden hairs on her arms. It appeared that everyone had tanned perceptibly since morning.

Marlene Miller, shiny with unguents, stretched on their deck in a bikini when they returned to the house. "Arnold won," she said.

"That's good," Scott said. Larry Silverman gazed at the sky and, crafty-eyed, observed, "Wind's getting around to the west."

Wind's getting around to the west – I should have said that, Scott thought. That was just the kind of thing he liked to say.

Barbara Feldstein strummed her guitar and sang, "Michael rowed the boat ashore, hallelujah..."

Scott emptied a quart of gin into a blue enamel coffee pot and added little bottles of tonic and slices of lime. Marlene Miller climbed the stairs dewy from a shower, prepared to fly in light, wind-blown clothes. Jennifer emerged in a short, white dress and it seemed to Scott that a hush fell upon the crowd.

"Come with us, Barbara," Scott said, but she shook him off. Art flashed him a look, as if to say, "Enough, enough." The coalition of the willing streamed out on a wooden walk leading to the sixish on Great South Bay.

A hum, as from a grain trading pit, rose from the assembled throng. Island regulars clogged center sand while newcomers circled at the edges.

Scott tried to hang back a step or two, to offer wit and support but not inhibit, as he and Jennifer wandered. It helped that he carried the coffee pot and that house members appeared and reappeared and extended empty glasses for him to fill. Across Great South Bay a huge, red sun dangled and prepared to make its nightly plunge.

Jennifer met a woman she knew. Scott slid away and pushed through people to the edge of the water. The sun teetered on the western horizon now and he thought he heard someone call his name. He turned. No, he must have imagined it, for the voice did not come from behind. The voice came from the sea.

Who, what, wanted his attention? What choices needed he make? Would the earth cease its rotation if he took a month off and lived in a cottage by the sea?

They argued politics and philosophy at dinner and Scott and Arnold Saperstein landed on opposite sides as if by instinct. Scott sought to assert his place in the sun: "Kant admits religion can't be proved, but yet he can't let go. Schopenhauer..."

"What's your point?" Arnold sliced in.

"I'm saying," Scott said, "that for two thousand years supposedly rational men erected elaborate philosophical systems and then dragged in god as an afterthought. I'm saying..." But another argument already ignited further down the table.

Still, he thought he saw in Jennifer's eyes that he acquitted himself well. They walked on the beach that night and sat and talked for over an hour high on a lifeguard stand.

Sunday morning arrived, clouds clumped and the wind smelled of rain. After two days and nights of group togetherness, Scott felt rhymed out. He did not want to throw the football, he did not want to sit and talk; he wanted to go home.

He and Jennifer rode the early afternoon boat to the mainland. They read the Sunday *Times*. They parted at Penn Station. "I'm sorry we didn't get the Celebrity Room," Scott said. "It seemed everything we did, we did in a crowd."

"That's what I expect in summer houses," Jennifer said.

They parted on a subway platform. "I'll call you," Scott said.

Jennifer eyed him, hands on her hips. "Do," she said.

❖　❖　❖

CHAPTER 12

"Good weekend?" Monica Corbin balanced on one high heel.

"Fine," Scott Lehmann said. "You?"

"We stayed in the city. We had it all to ourselves."

"'We?'"

"Bruce took me to The Cloisters and the Museum of Natural History."

"Them Golden Falcons make bad sounds," Barry Kalish said. He wore his usual Monday haggard, hangover look.

"Barry, what did you do?" Monica asked.

"I spent the weekend studying Tuttle, Osborn and Durkin research reports."

Telephones jangled. The squawk box barked buy recommendations. George Rogalski hunched in his office telephoning more clients on the recent RMF Properties offering.

"Look at him. He's pushing this one hard," Barry said.

"It pays a good commission," Scott said. He himself worked a bond offering that also rewarded brokers well. The market opened, yellow-green numbers skittered by, and an image of Jennifer Cohen in her swimsuit rose in his mind. Despite the crowding, the dorm-room situation over the weekend, she never lost her poise. He could not say that for himself.

He telephoned her office and she picked up the phone.

"Are you sitting down? *Shane* opens tonight at the Lincoln Plaza." Scott named a theater a few blocks north of Jennifer's apartment building.

"How many times have you already seen it?"

"Five, six; that's calibrated over months and years, of course."

"Why don't you just buy the video and watch it at home?"

"It's not the same. I'll bet you missed it first time around."

"You're right," Jennifer said. "I was four or five years old."

"How about tomorrow night?"

"I'll go, if you take me to dinner first."

Scott bounded up, pleased with himself, just as George Rogalski emerged bleary-eyed from his office. Probably *Night of The Trifids* played on the late show last night. Scott cuffed the older broker playfully on the shoulder. "George," he asked, "what do you want out of life?"

"I want to keep my kids off drugs and see them graduate from college."

"That's it?"

"I want to sit and stare at my wife at the breakfast table."

"There's no place you want to go?" Scott asked. "No mountain you want to climb?"

George scratched his chin, rubbed his head. He looked old today.

"I guess I would like new cedar siding for our house."

Scott harumphed and stomped about. Maybe I'll think like that too when I'm forty or fifty, he thought. Such goals seemed quaintly pedestrian to him now.

Tuesday after work he rode a subway north to Columbus Circle. The doorman glanced at him and said, "Ten C."

"Bravo," Scott responded. One previous visit and the man remembered.

Jennifer's apartment glowed like a happy cave with its books and stacks of records. She glided about on shiny, black high heels. Her black hair riffed and reriffed across her forehead.

They waited for the elevator. "I sent out some resumes today," she said. "For myself. I'll tell you about it."

They walked up Columbus Avenue and chose an outdoor table at a restaurant that looked like a former bank. It was a warm summer night and the sidewalk coagulated with people.

"I'm almost twenty-six years old," Jennifer said. "I'm tired of buying brokers' drinks. I want to sell things myself – products, not stocks. I think I'd be good at it."

"What kind of products?"

"Things they sell in stores. Things that come in packages. Marketing is the game; packaging is the name. It's advertising, it's intuition. It's a special skill."

"To make more money than you do now?"

"In time, sure, but it's not just the money. I need a challenge." She spoke sonorously. "I want responsibility."

Waving a glass of wine, she sketched her history. As a girl she took ballet and piano. As a high school senior she slept with a coffeehouse singer. In college she coveted a boy with a motorcycle. She dated only Jewish men during what she described as her "middle period." Now, "neo-eclectic," as she put it, she did not want to be typed as "Jewish," she did not want to be typed as anything.

"I'm confident within myself," she said, "but I recognize that having a corner office and twenty-two people answering to me is not The Answer. Suburban marriage, driving Tracy to gymnastics and Brandon to little league is not The Answer."

Scott refilled their wine glasses. "What is The Answer?"

Jennifer leaned close, squinted, nodded wisely. "I'll know when it comes along."

Scott excused himself to go to the mens' room. Tanned lotharios leaned thoughtfully on one elbow next to leggy women along a bar lined with white columns. Tables fronted what resembled a row of grilled tellers' cages. "I believe this building is a former bank," he said, when he returned and sat down.

Jennifer leaned, close this time, so that her forehead almost touched his. "Where do you see yourself five years from now?"

Scott spread his arms and inhaled the crackling feeling of New York City. "The summer I turned thirteen I worked at a roller rink in Grange, Illinois. Two other kids and I helped people put on their skates and the boss gave us each a dollar a night and let us skate for free. I talked the other kids into asking for two dollars a night. We went in together to present our case. He fired all three of us."

"What is this, another one of your parables?"

"I'm saying that these days I enjoy what I do. As far as I'm concerned, these are the golden years. I would, however, like a private office."

Jennifer brightened. "'Scott, I represent a nationally known brokerage firm that wants to staff it's flagship office...'"

He laughed. "Flagship office. Give me a break."

They strolled arm-in-arm to a movie theater at Broadway and 63rd. "Odd," Jennifer teased, "no ticket line."

The theater darkened. The Teton Mountains of Wyoming climbed on the screen. Shane – the actor, Alan Ladd – rides into the valley. He agrees to work for the homesteader, Van Heflin. The two men swing their axes, framed by snow clad peaks, and hew a stubborn stump to the ground. Jean Arthur, the sod-buster's pretty wife, and Brandon DeWilde, the impressionable son, observe and admire.

But cattlemen, those instinctive haters of homesteaders, appear in the night. "It's ours. We made this country." The villains, as in a Shakespeare tragedy, eloquently state their case.

Jack Palance, the cattleman's hired gun, taunts the homesteader called Reb on the muddy street of the heartbreak town. "I'm saying all you rebels are trash. I'm saying Robert E. Lee is trash." His six guns roar, Reb's body skids across the mud.

Children play and nervous horses sidle at Reb's funeral high on a hill, while the low laughter of cattlemen echoes from the saloon in the great spaces below.

Alan Ladd unwraps his guns. "A gun is just a tool, Miriam, no better, no worse, than the man who uses it."

The boy runs to town and watches wide-eyed the slow talk, the epic showdown. Shane, wounded, rides away into the night, the valley safe now for churches and schools. "Come back, Shane. Come back..."

In the boy's voice all lost America sighs.

Scott sat stunned. It was the lone man against the world that moved him, the idea that one man can make a difference. He and Jennifer walked out and crossed the street before he could speak.

"You don't see Shane getting old," Jennifer said. "You don't see the whiskey bottles and the grimebag hotels and Shane drooling his stories that nobody wants to hear."

"The scenery, the other characters, the magnificent moment..." Scott, the flatlander from Illinois, wandered still below the mighty Tetons, lost in the legends of the West.

They walked south along Central Park. "It might be fun to drive up to the Adirondacks Friday," Scott said, "since we're both between weekends on our summer houses."

"To do?"

"Climb Mount Marcy."

"Have you climbed it before?"

"No. I want to. It's the biggest mountain in New York State."

"Where would we stay?"

"First night a motel. Second night we'd camp out."

Jennifer walked along beside him for half a block without speaking. "What about a backpack?" she asked.

"I've got an extra; I've got a tent, sleeping bags. You'd need hiker boots, though."

"Is this a see-if-Jennifer-can take-it?"

"No, no," Scott said, "I wouldn't time you or anything like that. Hard work, yes; a challenging climb, but I foresee fun."

"Fun as in foolish."

"I really think you'd do well at this," Scott said.

"I have hiker boots, but I've never slept on the ground before. We would sleep on the ground, right?"

"We inflate our air mattress and sleep on those. Didn't you ever go to summer camp? Didn't they lead you out in the woods overnight?"

"Ha. We sang around the campfire and slept in screened cabins near the lake. I'm a Great Neck girl."

"All the more reason to do it."

"I might. Your eloquence motivates me."
"That's a yes?"
"Pending the weather forecast, of course."
"Great! Accolades to you, Great Neck girl."
"I know I'll regret this," she said.

CHAPTER 13

Jennifer waited Friday in sandals, shorts and t-shirt in front of her apartment building. She wore little makeup, Scott noticed as she hopped into his car, and she looked fine without it. They felt around for topics until they cleared the city and then both talked at once.

She had applied for a marketing position at mighty General Brands. Howard Leibowitz, the corporate executive who had organized her summer house, knew people at Bristol Myers, and at his recommendation she had also applied there.

"What if there's an earthquake?" she asked. "What about bears?"

"I see quicksand as our greatest danger," Scott said, then smiled to show he jested. "I'm a young broker and I know I've done wrong," he sang her the sugar trading song. He told her about watching the new World Trade Center grow. He told her about playing basketball in Greenwich Village with Brent Hall.

The Catskills climbed, forested, pinnacled, an impressive sight after Fifty-Seventh Street. The New York Thruway spanned high bridges over deep-cut, mystery streams. The Catskills fell behind and the thruway dipped into Albany's plains.

Friday traffic slowed at times to a crawl and heat waves rippled from seemingly endless double lines of cars. Nearing Albany, they turned toward Canada on the Northway and suddenly broke free. Dark, ominous ripples skimmed the horizon ahead. "The Adirondacks," Scott said. "Mountains without pity."

"I don't like the look of those clouds," Jennifer said, and Scott, for the first time, considered the possibility that something might actually go wrong. What if, despite favorable forecasts, it did rain? What if she sprained an ankle eleven miles from a road?

"It's not ordained that we climb Marcy," he said. "I mean, there are smaller mountains."

"You don't think I can do it?"

"I mean if a hurricane blows in, if the elements conspire against us." Scott shifted position, increasingly aware of Jennifer's brown, bare legs. They could do day hikes, he thought. They could eat in restaurants, tumble together in beds. They need not camp out at all.

"My reputation is on the line here," Jennifer said. "I told the people in my office I would climb Mount Marcy."

"Well then, by god, we will."

Darkness descended, pines ruled the night. They turned off the Northway onto the Lake Placid Road. "Getting close to Canada," Scott said. Jennifer snapped on the interior light to study a map and accidentally he triggered the parking blinkers. To cars behind, he thought, they probably looked like a jukebox hurtling north.

She cocked her head. "Say we do this, say we achieve our goals; what is my reward?"

"Inner peace," Scott said.

They rode quietly for a while. She pointed. "I see stars."

"That's a good sign, it must be clearing from the north. Good sighting, Jennifer."

They passed a restaurant and a few houses, the first settlement since the Northway, and Scott turned in at a motel sign. Old-timey cabins with screened porches squatted in a semicircle about fifty feet apart. Grass grew in the parking areas between.

"We used to stay in places like this when I was a kid," he said.

"How much further is Lake Placid?"

"Fifteen, twenty miles, but we don't go that far before we strike into the mountains tomorrow. Let's look at one of the cabins here."

A white-haired man handed them a key and they explored a cabin set away from the road. It looked clean. It offered a big double bed, a stove and a refrigerator. Jennifer ran her fingers across a table and patted the bed. "I'm game," she said.

They carried in their things. Scott made McNertneys, his term for Scotches and water, using ice from the refrigerator.

"What do you call a beer?"

"A Frondheim."

"You ought to consider a career in marketing," Jennifer said.

He carried two chairs outside to the grass. It was probably ninety degrees in the city and the coolness of summer night up here surprised them both. She slipped on a jacket, he draped a sweater. Shadowy mountains reared. The moon blazed brightly and its radiance fuzzed the edge of retreating clouds.

Scott jumped up, looked around inside their room and returned with a Gideon Bible. "I always wanted to try this." He opened the book to Ecclesiastes and read, "'Man goeth to his long home.' How about that? 'Man goeth to his long home.' That's death." He read more lines. "I'm reading by the light of the moon," he said. "You see? It can be done."

"I can die now," Jennifer said. "I've seen it all."

Scott stretched. She faced him, eyes shadowed, one barefoot leg across the arm of his chair. "What time do we get up?"

"Reasonable; seven, seven-thirty."

"It's past eleven," she said. "I read my watch by the light of the moon."

He laughed, she held the porch door and Scott in his eagerness bumped into her from behind. The top of her head came about to his chin.

"I'll do my girlish maneuvers." He heard water running and he congratulated himself that he had not, at Davis Park and in the city, tried to rush things. It's like skiing, he thought. You do best when you respect the mountain.

Jennifer emerged in a short, peppermint-stripe nightie and gracefully eased into bed.

Scott showered, brushed his teeth and padded out with a towel wrapped around his waist. She sat up in bed, pillow propped, studying a brochure. "According to this, the Adirondacks rank as the biggest state park in America."

Scott traced with his fingers on the map. "It's huge." All week he had anticipated and he found himself breathing erratically, as before a big game. He got in naked beside her and she put away the brochure.

"It won't be this comfortable tomorrow night, will it?"

"Sometimes the ground is soft. And we have our air mattress."

"How big is it?"

"About from our knees to our heads."

"I imagined us digging a trench around our tent to keep water out and sleeping on a bed of pine boughs."

Scott laughed. "That pine bough stuff never made sense. Bunch of Boy Scouts tearing up the forest."

"I'll just have a tiny bit more of that Scotch," Jennifer said.

Scott poured. He added a hefty splash to his own glass too. "I apologize for all my silliness out at Davis Park," he said. "You're the first date I asked out there. Feeling my way, so to speak."

"I learned about terminal moraines."

"Separate, communal rooms. Like freshman year in college."

"How big are our sleeping bags?"

"There's just one, but it's double size. Actually, I zipped two bags together.

"I'm ready to turn out the light," she said.

He jumped up, snapped the wall switch, and leaped back into bed. He imagined Jennifer in high heels and black stockings. He imagined her doing a saucy cheerleader step. He saw her dance for him in slow motion, her hair float out, her earrings swing. Stop imagining, he thought, here she is.

He peeled the peppermint nightie slowly upward.

"Whoops..." She chuckled.

"The King of Foreplay," he said. Moonlight slanted through a window and she extended one leg, toe pointed, the perfect thigh, the perfect ankle. She grasped him around the neck, digging in her fingers as if to provoke him, so he pushed her arms away and held her down. She struggled. He felt her fingernails on his back and he lifted her wrists above her head and held them there. Her breathing speeded. They twisted together.

"That's good. Right there," she said.

They tested; here, there, upward, downward. Her hips held him. He gripped her hands and lifted them above her head again and bore down harder and she shuddered as if she had been shot.

Scott lay quietly thinking of the many hours of his life he spent chasing women. He considered the energy, the time. Might he have done better to read history, to study mathematics? He should exercise more. The joy, after all, was to move, to be in motion. The moon made shadows, a breeze smelled of pines.

"Hey? Are you there?" Jennifer tugged verbally at his sleeve.

Grass shone with dew in the morning and the mountains seemed fresher and closer than they had in the night.

"Jennifer, come and see. The sky's so blue it hurts your eyes."

She stepped out, pretended to limp. "I've changed my mind about hiking. My foot hurts." She grinned. "I'm kidding, I'm kidding."

CHAPTER 14

"We need carbs," Scott said. He and Jennifer drove to a nearby restaurant and ladled guilt-free maple syrup on blueberry pancakes. Out-of-state cars nudged each other in the parking lot. They bought groceries at a store above a bounding stream and drove northwest on the Lake Placid Road.

The highway climbed. They passed two long, narrow lakes hemmed by trees, crossed a ridge, and the world opened. Peak after peak soared ahead, some bare and open on top, others rich with trees. One, dappled with floating clouds, rose higher than the others.

"Getting close," Scott said. They turned at a sign, "Adirondack Loj," and followed a dirt road to a small lake and a rustic hikers' dormitory at the edge of the mountains.

Jennifer pondered the rough-hewn building. "Could we hike up and down today and stay here tonight?"

"Not and do the grand tour." By starting early and hiking late they probably could summit and return in one day, but Scott wanted to explore the other side of the mountain. He wanted to traverse a mighty loop on the map. He wanted to cook over a campfire and to sleep in a tent. He wanted adventure.

He loaded the tent, sleeping bag and extra clothing in his pack, the food and utensils in Jennifer's. He lifted her pack and held it so she could slip her arms into the straps. He had borrowed it from Bruce Stanton, the Golden Falcon, and he felt like a foreign exchange student wearing it home in the subway after work.

He helped Jennifer adjust the straps. "How does it feel?"

She pretended to stagger.

"I could take some of that food in my pack."

"No, no, I'm fine. Really. It's not so bad."

They plunged into forest and Scott, a sun-lover, looked longingly up at snatches of blue sky. The trail tracked a stream, rose gently for two miles, and broke into sudden brightness at a small lake. They walked across a dam and rested at a picnic table bathed in sun.

"It's going to get worse, isn't it," Jennifer said. She looked like a model on an outdoor shoot with her spiffy boots, socks folded once and neatly aligned, shorts snug on toned thighs.

"It may get steeper. Pack feel all right?"

"Fine."

"You sure?"

"What would you do if I said no?"

"Throw up my hands. Frown."

They climbed the steep Phelps Brooks Trail, an old path that had eroded in places almost to a gully. Tree roots and rocks protruded and Scott, who thought himself in shape, felt the strain. They paused, breathing hard.

"Want me to take some of your load?"

Jennifer's socks had slithered lower. Drops of sweat trembled on her forehead. She dabbed at her face with a handkerchief and hoisted her socks. "Not yet. We'll see."

They climbed again and after what seemed an interminable pull burst free into sunlight and strolled out on a prong of rock. A stream jetted past in a glistening groove of stone and disappeared over a cliff. Mountains crowded close, the air felt thinner. Peaks that seemed distant and impersonal in the morning now developed faces and personalities.

Scott approached a hiker sitting nearby. "Where are we?" he asked.

"You're at Indian Falls, my friend."

They lolled in the sun and ate cheese and apples. The stream rushed past and flung itself into space. Jennifer lay on her back, eyes closed; he studied his map and sighted on a peak. "That's the Big One?" he asked the taciturn stranger.

"That's Colden. Keep climbing; Marcy will appear."

They toiled upward again but on a trail less steep than before. Trees looked shorter, more ravaged. It grew colder and puffball clouds rushed overhead. They topped over a ridge and stopped to stare; directly ahead, on the far side of a sudden valley, a massif of rock rose. It filled the sky and clouds whipped its top like smoke in the wind "Everest," Jennifer said, but Scott noted from her expression, her posture, that now she shared the drama of their quest.

The trail circled left and up, tracking a ridge through small and twisted trees. Then the trees ceased all together and the trail climbed into a zone of bushes and grass. It zigged, zagged, higher, higher, until it reached bare, broken rock.

The wind quickened and a dense, gray, moistness enveloped them, shutting off all view of the world below. Scott and Jennifer clambered over bare rock until they saw no higher place to go. An eerie brightness raced up the slope, closer, closer, until suddenly the wind ripped the mist away.

They stood on the highest spot for hundreds of miles and gazed across green distances at mountains and more mountains and lakes that shone like puddles in the sun. Around them other hikers emerged from nooks and crannies where they had sheltered from the wind. They smiled, exclaimed, gestured at far horizons.

Scott grinned at Jennifer and lifted his arms in celebration. "Fifty-three hundred and some feet. Not much by Rocky Mountain standards."

"Of course, you start lower in the East," she said.

"Good point." Scott looked at her appreciatively and without warning a mist like cold smoke, darker than the previous cloud, rushed upslope and enveloped them. They crouched to avoid the bite of the wind.

"Jesus." Scott rummaged for plastic slickers he had stuffed into his pack. They helped each other pull them on and crawled beneath an overhanging rock.

"What time is it?" he asked. Jennifer wore a watch.

"Two-twenty-four."

Scott shivered in sudden cold. "We should get going soon. We've got a ways to go," he said.

She thinks I know what I'm doing, he thought. She thinks I climb mountains like this all the time. He planned this hike in the comfort of his New York City apartment, visualizing well-tended trails, a campsite with views. It had looked easy, sitting at home.

Scott peered out from under their ledge. "Still raining. What the hell? Let's go."

Picking their way, they followed white blazes painted on rock down Marcy's west flank, opposite the way they had climbed. Scott guessed that most of the other hikers would probably descend the other way, back the well-traveled route.

Piles of stones also marked this trail. Rain stung their faces. The rock slanted in slippery slabs but seemed easier going than the jumbled riff-raff on top. The mists parted for a moment, and in that moment Scott glimpsed a slanting line of trees below.

"We're progressing," he called back.

They descended into these trees and the trail dropped steeply into a high-walled valley. Rain laced this chasm like rivulets of steam. Peering down, Scott experienced a strange excitement; we'll remember this, he thought. He looked back; Marcy had disappeared into cloud.

"There's a body of water down in that valley called Lake Tear of the Clouds. I thought we might camp there."

"Lake Tear of the Clouds." Jennifer caressed the words. "Sounds good to me."

They sloshed down a steep path that in this storm became a stream bed. A valley floor rose toward them. Jennifer walked in front, hair wet, face dripping. She's doing it, Scott thought. She's not complaining.

The rain slowed to desultory drops by the time they reached the valley floor. Scott unfolded his map: Panther Gorge lay to the left, Lake Tear of the Clouds to the right. They turned right and walked in muddy ooze.

He anticipated an idyllic mountain lake. They rounded a bend and saw ahead a marshy pond covered with algae. Jennifer stopped. "Lake Tear of the Clouds?"

"I'm afraid so." Indeed it was, a rain-darkened sign confirmed.

Bad enough, the aesthetics. Worse, Scott scanned the shores of this fetid place and saw no suitable campsite. It neared five o'clock. His ankles hurt and he knew Jennifer was tired. He pondered his map. "A stream flows from here down to the Opalescent River and our trail pretty much parallels the stream. Let's walk and look. All we need is a level place for the tent."

They splashed through mud. Trees tangled together. Rock and stump holes pocked the ground. They had carried their packs up the biggest mountain in New York State and down the other side and all they needed now was a flat spot to put their tent. But the further they walked down this dripping valley the more rugged the terrain became.

"Unbelievable," Scott said.

They plodded on, hardly speaking. At least the rain had stopped.

"What time now?"

"Twenty to seven." It would grow dark, in early July, at about nine, Scott calculated.

They slogged down this muddy trail and he spotted something white through the trees. The Opalescent River? He rushed forward, snapping branches. Yes! He saw boulders and green, tumbling water. He stood on a stretch of flat ground beneath a Garden of Eden grove of pines.

Jennifer followed. They flopped on pine needles, slipped off their packs. "How far do you think we came?"

"Twelve, thirteen miles," Scott said. "Hard miles," he added.

They heard a splashing. Two hikers carrying bright orange packs hurried in the fading light along the muddy trail. "We found our cave," Scott said. "They're still looking." He and Jennifer had done it, so would these others. He watched the orange packs disappear. He did not feel like sharing; what he felt was pride.

"You look for firewood," he said. "I'll put up the tent."

He erected their new home on a bed of pine needles while Jennifer gathered dead branches that lay all around on the ground. Scott shaved twigs for kindling, wadded a paper bag, lit a match and fed gradually larger twigs into the blaze. The paper bag went out. He rummaged in his pack and found a square of newspaper. This time the fire caught.

He poured cups of Scotch and they dangled their bare feet in the cold, green water of the Opalescent River. The planet Venus appeared in the western sky. The fire popped behind them. Why did he love this so? Scott wondered.

"I suspect, had I not met you, that I might have gone through life and never climbed Mount Marcy," Jennifer said.

"It's a first for me too. I'm excited."

She sliced and salted celery and radishes, tasted, and rolled her eyes. He barbecued steaks on the open fire. "Everything tastes gourmet when you camp along the Opalescent River," he said.

They ate facing the flames. Scott collected their utensils when they finished and scrubbed them with gravel in the river. Kneeling, his hands in the cold water, he glanced back at their camp. Jennifer sat knees to chin, eyes shadowed, surrounded by dark forest.

He refilled their cups with a teak-colored mixture of whiskey and water. Jennifer sipped. "You think it would help if I put this trip on my resume?"

He laughed, prepared to laugh at anything. "Where would you rather wind up, General Brands or Bristol Myers?"

"Either, or. Actually, I suppose General Brands, because then I start fresh, I don't owe anyone. I told you Howard Leibowitz set up my interview at Bristol Myers."

"Did you two used to go out?"

"Why do you ask?"

"Your tone. The cut of your jib."

"Yes," she said, "Howard and I were companions last summer."

"That's kind of awkward," Scott said, "both of you still in the same summer house."

"It happens." Wind rustled the trees and Jennifer cocked her head and looked behind. She turned to Scott. "What about you and Marlene what's-her-name?"

"Marlene Miller. I'll admit, at first I had designs. But it's a long, active line."

They talked softly, staring at the fire. The Opalescent River gurgled over stones. Fits of breeze sighed through the trees. "Sky's still clearing, bodes good for tomorrow," Scott said. "See. Here comes the moon."

They watched it rise from a ridge, rest for a moment and break free. They yawned, they stretched, and Jennifer announced her intention to crawl inside the sleeping bag. "Show me what to do."

Scott demonstrated zippers on the bag and the mosquito netting of the tent.

"Do I wear anything?" she asked.

"Whatever's comfortable. You won't need much."

She stripped to her panties, neatly folding each piece of discarded clothing.

"Use your sweater for a pillow," Scott suggested.

"Good idea." She wiggled into the sleeping bag.

Scott drank a cup of icy water from the Opalescent River and took a last look at the woods. Blissfully weary, he squirmed in naked beside Jennifer and watched the glow of the dying fire dance on the tent.

A sexual itch announced itself and took shape. He touched the woman beside him. She sighed and flung an arm, already asleep.

Scott watched through the thin fabric of the tent as the moon moved across the sky. Twigs popped in the trees. A bear? More likely a porcupine. He slept and awoke and noticed that the moon declined into the tops of trees. He needed to urinate, and he crawled out barefoot into the night.

He brushed pine needles off one foot, then the other, and slid back into the sleeping bag. He slept, he awoke again, and he thought he heard someone call his name. He listened; yes, he heard the voice distinctly. He touched Jennifer, but she lay drugged in sleep.

He crawled outside and gazed up, startled, at the sky. Green banners, separated as in a giant fan, spread swiftly southward above the mountains. They looked like streamers, living streamers, and as he watched they advanced from the north, quavered, retreated, and advanced again. They filled the sky like endless stripes of a pulsating, celestial flag. He watched, mesmerized.

The northern lights. The aurora borealis. He had seen this only once before, on a January night in Vermont. But how could it happen in July? I must awaken Jennifer, he thought. But the green banners began to retreat. They halted, started forward again in a last desperate try, failed, and unraveled backward into blackness.

Scott became aware of his bare feet sticky again with pine needles. He brushed them off and stood on a flap of the tent, hoping the banners would advance again. But the northern lights did not return.

He crawled back inside the sleeping bag and lay listening. He had read, and forgotten, scientific explanations for the aurora borealis. But who, what had called his name?

He told Jennifer in the morning of his adventures in the night. It all seemed remote now in bright summer sun.

"I wish you had yelled and rousted me out."

"So strange. I distinctly heard someone call."

"'Scott?' Someone called, 'Scott?'"

"Yes. I got up and stepped outside and that's when I saw the lights."

"Maybe I called. You know, a fantasy..."

"It seemed to me that the voice came from further." But he smiled, to honor what she had said. He slung on his pack and glanced around at this home they would never see again. The stream fluted to its own dancing music, grass and trees groped toward the sun.

They followed a trail down the Opalescent River. Mud and puddles lingered from yesterday's rain and flecks of brown speckled Jennifer's socks and legs. Scott noticed how her expression changed with the terrain; alert, serene, annoyed, depending on the footing.

She stopped and stared down at the Opalescent River. "Now this is amazing."

He stopped beside her and looked down through clear water. Little fish glided along the bottom and stones six feet deep appeared magnified to boulder size.

They walked on. The river thundered through crevices, skidded beneath fallen trees, calmed itself in limpid pools. Then, suddenly, the trail opened and mountains reared above as if they stood in Switzerland.

Celebrating, the Opalescent River cleared its chasm and burst into Lake Colden.

They walked around the south end of this lake and every thirty yards produced another view. The trail left the water and climbed into woods. "Drama," Scott said. He knew from the guidebook that Avalanche Lake waited ahead.

High cliffs rose abruptly from this deep, narrow, glacier-carved tarn. Sheens of water glittered on rock faces above. The trail appeared to vanish into cliffs, a trap, no place to go.

They approached and saw the solution; log ladders led over rocks and wooden walks spanned stretches of deep, clear water.

Scott heaved his way up a ladder. "You wouldn't want to be an a hurry coming through here." He wondered if Jennifer would at last complain.

"That's for sure."

Dry ground. A final ridge remained, and then a relatively gentle four-mile descent to their car. They climbed to a gap in a wall of rock where a trickle of water spattered down. Scott read from the Adirondack Mountain Club guidebook, "'...This marks the northernmost source of the Hudson River...'"

He pictured this same river 250 miles south, shaping Manhattan, three miles wide at Tappan Zee. He glanced down at the trickle at his feet. He nudged a rock with his toe. "Let's dam it."

Jennifer appeared startled, as if picturing stranded, flopping fish, the vast riverbed of the Hudson empty. "We'd better not," she said.

They decided to let the water flow unimpeded and, in what became the longest and sorest miles of their weekend, hiked a sloping green tunnel out to civilization. Their talk turned toward the long drive home, the city, Monday morning.

Scott drove the dirt road out to the main highway, stopped and hopped out of the car. "A last look." Already he strained to recapture the mood, the sound, the teasing urgency of the voice that called to him in the mountains.

High peaks slanted in the sun. He gestured toward them. "They were here when we were born. They will be here when we die."

"So will Park Avenue," Jennifer said. "Come on. Let's go home."

This IS home, Scott started to say. But he did not, the moment passed. He pointed his car south toward New York City.

CHAPTER 15

"She called me at my office. She said she heard I applied to law school at Eugene, Oregon. Did you tell her?"

"Not me, no, no."

"Who then?"

"I don't know. Larry Silverman, maybe. She likes you, Lamont."

"Barbara Feldstein? Come on, Storm." Scott Lehmann and Art Levin idled in the sun on the steps of the Federal Building. A young women in high heels bought hotdogs from a street vendor and sat on the steps below.

"Witches cauldron, devils' brew; I wish I had a hotdog too," Art leaned and said. The woman turned and crinkled a smile.

"Adroitly done, Lamont."

"That headhunter you brought out to the island, she's adroit."

"The elusive Jennifer. Last weekend we slept in a tent in the Adirondacks and climbed Mount Marcy."

"I didn't think they made hairdryer extension cords that long."

"Au contrare, Lamont, it rained, we hiked miles in mud. We're talking heroism here."

Art looked skeptical. "I want to stay posted on this."

"So what's this about the University of Oregon. You applied? You filled out the forms and all that stuff?"

"I applied to Oregon and to law schools in the New York area as well. Not wanting to stir anxiety, I did not mention the Far West to my parents. I've set the wheels in motion, Storm."

"And now with Barbara, as with ripples on a pond, the repercussions spread. She's worried, Lamont. She's worried that you will leave."

"Larry probably told her. He asked me if I wanted to join the house again next summer. Did he call you? He will. I said I didn't know and foolishly let slip the word 'Oregon.'" Art rose and dusted his pants. "Cursed job: this afternoon another grungy landlord."

They descended the steps of the Federal Building and turned their separate ways. Scott purchased a cup of tea and an apple raisin muffin to carry back to his desk.

Four or five brokers clustered outside George Rogalski's office. Scott approached Monica Corbin. "What's doing?" He knew that George's wife had called earlier to say he did not feel well and would not come in today.

"I don't know. Walter wants to see you and Barry."

Scott hunted up Barry and the two of them walked into Walter Cappaletti's office. Walter sat them down and stared fixedly out his window at New York Harbor. "It's cancer," he said. "He's unconscious, he's in a hospital, and it's spread to his brain."

"Cancer?"

"What cancer?"

"Melanoma. He's had it for years. That's why he wore his hair cut so short; the doctors told him to do that so he could spot any unusual growth. Okay, here's the situation: I've decided to divide George's accounts between you two until he comes back. Someone has to service them. I know you won't mind if the commission payouts go to his wife."

"Can we visit him in the hospital?" Scott asked.

"As soon as he regains consciousness," Walter said.

George's wife called from the hospital two days later and said he wanted to speak with Scott on the telephone. "How are you, young broker?" Scott heard a quavering, almost unrecognizable voice. He visualized tubes, vials, cold white walls.

"Now pay attention..." The shaky, distant voice named several of his larger accounts. "...I want you to take them on condition that if I die – no, hear me now – that if I die one half of all commissions go to my wife for the next three years. I want this in writing."

"You'll be back, George. You'll be back."

"I want you to take them. Do you agree?"

"I agree. Can we come see you?"

"Maybe. Right now I just want to go home."

Scott descended the hill to the Rector Street subway later that afternoon. Summer sun glinted on the new Trade Center towers and a soft breeze blew in from New York Harbor. There must be some mistake, Scott thought. Nothing's changed, nothing at all.

George Rogalski died six days later.

His wife, still in her forties, thanked them for coming to the wake. She moved as if distracted, strangely bright-eyed, desperately composed. George lay silent and still in an open coffin, youthful in his crewcut. Brokers from the office passed to look at him and filed to a corner where drinks awaited. George's children appeared briefly.

"We'll miss him," Scott said to the wife. He saw no change in her expression. She shook his hand. She fought to retain her composure.

She knew that though her husband, the father of her children, had died, the stock market would open as usual tomorrow.

Walter Cappaletti moved Scott into George's office with its view of the Statue of Liberty and the new World Trade Center towers. Barry Kalish got a similar office next door and Monica Corbin a new and larger desk outside and halfway between.

Scott sat at his new desk twenty-four floors up, view to the south – it seemed he could see 50 miles. Walter summoned him and Barry. "All right, you guys, you got offices of your own and you each got some of George's accounts. Should you feel pressure to produce? Yes. Should you worry? Yes. The selling of securities is a stress occupation. If you wanted dull jobs you should have gone into the civil service."

Scott examined the accounts he had inherited from George and noticed that many had recently invested in RMF Properties. He called them one by one to introduce himself and to inform them, if they did not already know, of the circumstances of George's death. He found that many knew virtually nothing about RMF Properties, and had learned of their investment only when the confirmation arrived in the mail.

RMF had paid an unusually high commission and Scott remembered that George had pushed the offering hard. "Taking care of his wife; I understand," one client said. But neither this client or any of the others officially complained or asked that their RMF purchases be rescinded. They all seemed to realize that George sensed the advance of his cancer, and that before he died he tried to provide his family with one last big payday. Because they had liked George, they did not complain. Maybe RMF would turn out to be a good investment, they said.

Scott told Jennifer Cohen about it over glasses of wine at dinner. He arrived at the restaurant first, ordered a drink at the bar and waited among wood and mirrors and gliding waiters. He watched her make her entrance in her usual dark skirt, white blouse and shiny shoes. Something different, he noticed: tonight she wore a wide, rigid-looking leather belt with a silver buckle.

"George's customers really respected him," Scott said. "I want them to feel that way about me too."

"What happens to his family?"

"Barry and I split commissions on George's old accounts with his wife for the next three years."

"You both got your private offices?"

Scott noticed that everyone seemed to comment on that. "I think we would have gotten them anyway, sooner or later."

"What kind of cancer was it?"

He offered details. George's crewcut – the fact that he wore it for so many years – seemed especially significant to them both.

"I've news too," Jennifer said. "Shake hands with the new assistant vice president, marketing, General Brands."

He kissed her on the cheek. "A title already? Come on."

"The future, in one word?" Jennifer looked expectant. Scott waited. Had he missed something? "Ask me," she said.

"The future in one word?"

"Packaging," she said.

"Ah. Of course."

"With proper packaging, with carbon dioxide, it is possible to keep sticky buns fresh for six months. You can brown food, you can create those neat grill lines on fish. How, you wonder? Because General Brands' new packages include magic devices called metal receptors. GB products offer marvels only dreamed of by the owners of ratty, old microwaves."

"No one can accuse you of a lack of enthusiasm," Scott said.

"The white coats develop this stuff in the laboratory. My job is to move it off the shelves."

"Where is General Brands?"

"Park Avenue. Uptown."

"Uptown," he repeated. He knew that's where she wanted to be.

But they rode a taxi downtown this sultry, summer night because Scott wanted to show Jennifer a new Village bar called Green Sleeves. They got out at Sheridan Square.

"What's so special about Green Sleeves?"

"The *Times* did a piece," Scott said. "The *Village Voice* did a piece. It attracts painters and writers. It's a seething hotbed of creativity."

"You're sure it's not where the Swedish woman's drill team trolls for guys? I'm kidding, I'm kidding."

"The wit light is on," Scott started to say, but a burst of noise erupted across the street and he and Jennifer turned to look. A group of men dressed in leather clustered in front of a saloon on Christopher Street. "Overflow from the Iron Man," Scott said. This was a bar often mentioned in the tabloids as a hangout for homosexuals.

He looked again. That dark avenger in black leather, casual against a parking meter, looked a lot like Barry Kalish. It *was* Barry Kalish, and without thinking Scott lifted his hand in greeting. Barry saw him, and disappeared inside the Iron Man.

"Somebody you know?" Jennifer asked.

"He looked like somebody from our office."

"A broker?"

"I think so." Scott left it at that. They found seats along the bar at Green Sleeves, three blocks further north, and swiveled to survey the scene. Couples not unlike themselves composed tonight's crowd and the prints and paintings on the walls had the look of throw-offs from an apartment store bargain basement.

Jennifer crossed her legs. She seemed coiled tonight; eager. "What time do the painters and writers get here, do you think?"

"Well, it's a Wednesday."

"I suppose it's sheer chance you live near here."

"By gosh, that's right: you haven't seen my apartment."

They dined. They walked briskly up Bleecker to Eighth Avenue. "Just ten more blocks," Scott said. Jennifer sighed and fanned her face. "An elevator," she said in mock surprise. They rode to the sixth floor. He showed her his bookshelves and his liquor cart on wooden wheels, manufactured in Mexico.

"Come see." He led her to a window. The Empire State Building rose center stage, its tapered spire illuminated tonight, as every night, in spectral glow.

"Drama for a boy from Illinois," Scott said. "I've seen lightning strike it twice."

She peered into his bedroom. "I wonder if lightning ever strikes in here."

"With luck, perhaps it may strike tonight."

Jennifer snorted, and examined his kitchen. "Get some good cleanser, not this stuff." She reclined on the couch and stretched her black-stockinged legs.

He lowered the lights and played rueful, confessional songs on the phonograph. They kissed and she bit his lip. "What do suppose those guys in leather do?" she asked.

"Let's experiment." Scott unhooked her wide, leather belt, fixed it tightly around her ankles, and carried her into the bedroom.

CHAPTER 16

Scott Lehmann arrived early at the office and found Barry Kalish already there. I'll act natural, Scott thought. I won't tell him where I saw him last night. He poked his head in Barry's door. "Interest rates?" he asked.

"Bonds up, the yen's down."

Scott flicked on his computer and checked the morning's news. "Interesting item on the news ticker," he called. The item had to do with productivity and it was as dull as sand.

Barry appeared at Scott's door. "What's with you today?" he asked.

"What do you mean?"

"You're unctuous."

Scott studied his colleague and tried to imagine he had never seen him before. He saw a tall, frizzy-haired man of 30 who dressed well, who looked intelligent, who seemed in decent physical condition. Would a woman be attracted? Sure, why not? Would a man?

Monica Corbin strolled by and Barry stared her up and down. "Monica, you're gorgeous today," he said. She stopped, surprised.

Enough, Scott thought, I must end this. Barry seemed to grasp his intent and he stepped into Scott's office. "Big deal, you saw me last night outside the Iron Man. I thought you knew."

"All that talk about Scandinavian airline stewardesses," Scott said.

"Stewards. Not stewardesses." This was it? They might be discussing a new utility stock offering.

"Who else in the office knows?" it occurred to Scott to ask.

"One for sure. He works in the order room."

"Nathan?"

"Andre," Barry said.

Barry's phone rang once, twice. Monica, busy with someone on another line, hesitated in picking up the new call. Barry grabbed his phone, listened, and flung it down. "Monica, goddamn it, tell goddamn Bruce to call you at home." Back to normal, Scott thought.

Moving numbers raced by. "Scott, Mrs. Lander," Monica called.

"Hello, Scott, how are you today? I want to sell my Princeton Group."

Scott checked the Pink Sheets for a current quote. "It's seventy cents bid, Mrs. Lander." He opened a loose leaf ledger in which he grouped less active accounts and saw that she had purchased her thousand shares at exactly that price.

"My friend says she sold hers for a dollar. Let's put it in to sell for a dollar, please, Scott."

He entered the order. These small accounts took more time than they were worth but he hated to let them go. Maybe when Monica got registered he'd pass his little people on to her.

Brent Hall called and suggested basketball after work at the outdoor court in Greenwich Village.

"It will be turgid," Scott said. Temperature's supposed to hit ninety."

"All the better," Brent said.

The shadow of the movie theater almost crossed Sixth Avenue at six o'clock but sun still blasted the concrete court across the street. Players in headbands raced from one metal rim to the

other and back again while an ever-changing audience of passersby leaned on the wire fence to watch.

A black kid bumped Brent and stole the basketball. Brent hooked
him and stole it back. Scott, open downcourt, yelled to catch his
eye, but the kid swung an elbow and grabbed for the ball again.
Brent shouldered him away and clung to the ball. It energized Scott
just to watch him. His friend staked his life on every game.

They sprinted up and down the court, won some and lost
some, while unnoticed the sun slid slowly from view. Darkness
crept in on sweaty sneakers and in grateful twilight something
approaching consummation settled over the trees and rooftops
of Greenwich Village.

Scott bounced Brent's basketball down West Fourth Street.
Seekers from uptown, downtown, all around eddied through
Sheridan Square ahead of them as if caught in a whirlpool, quick-
ening as they neared the entrance to Christopher Street.

"'Them,'" Brent said.

"Yes." Scott saw himself in the Paris of Hemingway's novel.
In the morning Jake Barnes would go to his office and get off
some cables.

He and Brent ordered steamer clams and a pitcher of sangria at an outdoor restaurant. The waitress, harried in the heat,
punched down their water glasses as if placing banderillas.

"Full house tonight," Scott attempted conversation as she
hurried past.

"Tell me about it." She rushed on.

Scott turned to Brent. "You have the poem?" Inspired by Art
Levin at a chance encounter on the steps of the Federal Building,
Brent entered a bad poetry contest sponsored in jest by another
textbook firm. To his credit, or dishonor, he won.

Brent read, in a conversational tone: "Life against death? Aye,
tormented sea. Hurl not your thunderbolt of anger, at me..."

He paused, wet his fingers. "Long the Great Divide pale
silence weeps, unrepenting Sierra snows. Beck not, dishonor,
silvered fate; shameward I dare not go. Born but to die, glory
seek it we; downward, downward, artificial muse, childlike seek
victory."

A hush settled around them. Brent modestly eyed the basketball on the table. Scott broke the spell. "Yes. You've done it there."

"I read it to Ruth."

"And?" Scott knew Ruth now as the speech therapist from Queens.

"She smiled. I'm still a hillbilly, but now I'm an ironic hillbilly."

Scott stroked his chin. "'Downward, downward, artificial muse,'" he repeated. Who knew? He reflected on the good badness of what his friend had done.

"I took her to see the folk singer, Odetta. We smoked some pot." Brent's eyes focused afar, as if on a distant fence line across the Oklahoma plains.

"She's willing then?"

"For that, and more."

Scott waited for the more. "You'll be seeing her again?"

"That's the plan."

They walked up Seventh Avenue in the warm night, passing ragged, homeless men. Scott described how he and Jennifer Cohen climbed Mount Marcy. Brent stopped twice, fumbled in his pocket, and produced dollar bills for the vagrants.

Two days later Scott carried a rectangular brown package into the subway and up the stairs at Rector Street. He glanced, as he did every day, at the new Trade Center towers, and climbed the hill past Alexander Hamilton's grave.

Monica Corbin circled. "What have you there?"

"A picture I found in a used book store." Scott, who still felt presumptuous walking into George Rogalski's old office, unwrapped his package, a reproduction of a large painting by the Montana artist of the early 1900s, Charles M. Russell. He pounded a nail and hung the picture on the wall over his desk.

The painting depicted three mountain men on horseback silhouetted against the sky on the crest of a sagebrush ridge. A band of mounted Indians approached. One, apparently their leader, raised his hand to the white men, maybe to ask their destination, perhaps to seek tribute. A blue river coiled through cottonwoods below. Sky and space opened beyond the river, and beyond a line of blue-gray mountains.

Monica studied it, hands on her hips. Barry Kalish entered and burst into song, "Home, home on the range…"

"Okay, enough of this deviltry. Barry, I missed the morning call; what's the prognosis for the market?"

"Let's look to our firm's technical analyst for the answer." Barry read aloud from a mimeographed sheet: "'…One has to be impressed by the skepticism of the advisory services and the media's reluctance to endorse the upward trend. On the other hand we see lagging volume, phase G characteristics, a market that has gone nearly a year without a serious correction…'"

"What is he saying?" Scott asked.

"He is saying the market might go up or it might go down."

"So maybe we should buy or maybe we should sell."

"That's it," Barry said.

Scott studied technical charts and research reports. He missed George Rogalski. Monica turned in her chair. "Scott, the Bank."

Mr. Crosland wanted to put idle money to work, Ingrid Henson said, and she entered buy orders on several stocks for him, Mr. Irvin and herself. All told, she invested over three hundred thousand dollars; the commissions alone would pay Scott's rent for several months. He entered the orders and his telephone rang. It was Jennifer Cohen. "Want to join me this weekend at my group house in Amagansett?"

"Hmm." She had hinted she might invite him. "Accommodations?" Scott asked. He recalled the college dorm situation they stumbled into at his house on Fire Island.

"I called Howard and reserved the Purple Room."

"What if somebody else gets there first?"

"Trust me," Jennifer said.

CHAPTER 17

"What time did you leave the city?" They ask this question in summer houses around the world, Scott Lehmann thought. He heard, "What time did you leave the city?" every time somebody new walked in Friday night at Jennifer Cohen's group house in Amagansett.

Tales of raw horror abounded. It took Scott and Jennifer three and a half hours to drive ninety miles. Later arrivals muttered, in clenched- teeth tones, of shake-your-fist gridlock on the Long Island Expressway and Route 27.

House organizer Howard Liebowitz, sandy-haired, athletic, hugged Jennifer and called her "Jen." He shook Scott's hand and referred the two of them to an upstairs chamber known as "The Purple Room."

Jennifer led the way. A pillow stitched with the words, "Lawyers make better lovers," sprawled like a hopeful peder- ast on a double bed. She lobbed it aside. "Lawyers make more noise," she said.

Sheets and blankets awaited, neatly folded. Scott peered from a window at the lights of houses, closer, more orderly than the haphazard dune whimsy of Davis Park. He described the distant cracking of waves as "muted, not that aggressive, Davis Park thunder."

"'Muted.' That's not a word you usually hear in Amagansett."

They had space and privacy and Jennifer bounded about. She stripped to her bra and changed to a wrap-around dress, black stockings and flat, shiny shoes. "Yes, wear that." She approved Scott's floppy slacks and vertically-striped shirt.

They descended into the maelstrom and she introduced Scott around. As at Davis Park, it seemed everyone worked at exciting, challenging jobs and had attended only the top ten schools.

"Stockbroker, eh, got any hot tips?" a man asked Scott.

"Buy Cuban Railroads," Scott said. Jennifer laughed, as if relieved. "And quickly," she put in.

Howard Liebowitz, Jennifer's companion of the previous summer, asked about her new job at General Brands. He touched her shoulder and removed an imaginary bit of lint. "Room okay?" he asked.

"Except for that pillow left over from the Chicago World's Fair," Jennifer said.

"Why not, 'Ombudsmen make better lovers,'" Scott said.

"Ombudsman, yes," Howard dutifully chuckled. "Going sightseeing?" he asked. They edged toward the door.

"We'll start at The Shed and kind of work from there," Jennifer said.

They drove traffic-clogged Route 27 into the Village of Amagansett. "First the Cuban Railroads, then the ombudsman; did you eat carrots for lunch?" Jennifer said.

"Wheat germ for breakfast," Scott said. He remained, he knew, a stranger in paradise; one day you might hit a home run, the next you strike out four times.

The Shed, a sprawling, white building, resembled an old, often remodeled house. "Park anywhere you can," Jennifer said. People holding drinks crowded the bar/restaurant's porch, milled about on its lawn and spilled out into the street.

Scott leaned against a wall inside, legs spread for balance, surprised at the crush of people. Jennifer grinned and leaned overtly against him. "Jesus, Jennifer." An image leaped to Scott's mind:

her bending, muddy-legged, peering down into the depths of the Opalescent River.

A jukebox boomed, he suggested they dance and they inched a step left, a step right, no choice in this throng but to shuffle as if welded together. He caught a glimpse of the two of them in a mirror. His brown hair looked pasted down and yellowish from summer sun. She calmly studied the crowd over his shoulder.

They drove to another bar as crowded as the first. They danced, they drank more gin and tonic. "What's Gantry's like?" Scott remembered that someone at the house mentioned Gantry's.

"Like this," Jennifer said. "They're all like this."

But they wanted to dance and they drove to Gantry's and liked the music and it was past midnight when they left.

The living room at the house appeared empty and Scott followed a pair of shiny shoes up the stairs. They entered their room and heard voices outside and below. "Let's not turn on the light," Jennifer whispered. "Some of them sit out there on the patio at night."

Conspirators, they eased off their clothes in darkness. Scott lay on the bed naked, a little drunk, conscious of a breeze through the window. He reached out his arm and Jennifer bit him in the neck.

She fought him. Of course he knew by now that she liked to be forced. They tussled until gradually her muscles begin to relax. She felt scalding when finally he eased himself in. She uttered a brief, high-pitched yip and for a moment conversation ceased outside.

Scott heard the distant murmur of waves. People began to talk again.

The sun shone Saturday morning, no small thing when twenty people in a summer house contemplate how to spend their day. Scott and Jennifer broke early from the pack. They played tennis, changed from whites to swimsuits, and trudged over a sand hill to the ocean. A breeze flecked the water and fish-scale clouds lazed in the July sky – already a darker blue, Scott maintained, than in the blazing light of June.

They bodysurfed incoming waves and lay on their blanket. "Did you and Howard live together in the city?"

"I've never lived with a man. I have friends who do, who move in with somebody as casual as they change sanitary napkins. Not me; I can't think of a bigger decision."

"It might be instructional, to give it a week, say."

Jennifer flashed him a look and rolled onto her back. Sunlight furred her arms with little, golden hairs. "Why rush?" she asked.

"Well...," he said.

"What did you have in mind, my place or yours?"

"I'm just saying the idea has its interesting aspects."

She rolled up on her elbow to face him. "Okay. Let's say we still like each other three or four months from now. Let's talk about it then. Make sense?"

"Makes sense," Scott said.

They went for a long walk on the beach. Her housemates planned a big, sit-down Saturday night dinner, and Scott regarded it as an act of trust when Howard assigned him and Jennifer to purchase the lobsters.

They drove to a seaside shack and chose red, lively pound-and-a-halfers from a crowded tank. Scott winced at the rubber bands they wore on their claws. "Not good," he said, "a lobster's life."

"Hopefully they had good times before they got caught."

Other shopping squads sallied forth seeking decent wine at under ten dollars a bottle and corn on the cob fresh from the field. Everyone changed for dinner and made themselves big, clinking drinks. Howard left and returned with a willowy young Japanese woman.

Someone turned on the television. President Richard Nixon, seeking reelection against Democrat George McGovern, pledged to end the war in Vietnam that he inherited from Lyndon Johnson. The announcer described this conflict as "America's loss of innocence," igniting a flurry of responses from around the room.

"I thought the quiz show scandals cost us our innocence."

"Prohibition."

"Teapot Dome."

"General Grant's charge at Cold Harbor," Howard Liebowitz offered.

Scott, seeing a chance to establish himself as a prairie thinker, cleared his throat. "America lost its innocence when the first settlers speculated in land and killed Indians."

Someone nodded. Scott sensed eyes turned toward him.

Dinner talk turned to takeovers and Wall Street legerdemain. "Adventurers doing deals," he jumped out front again.

"Yes, but don't you think it's healthy, putting the old hidebound managements on notice that they must do better?" Howard Liebowitz eyed his farm-state successor.

"Healthy," Scott said, "if the shareholders don't suffer."

Howard brightened, as if this were the opening he hoped for, and Scott recalled with a sodden flash his inept philosophizing during Jennifer's visit to Davis Park. But Howard's date, the lovely Japanese, stepped in inadvertently to rescue him. Shifting the subject, she assaulted America's worship of growth while its inner cities schools fell apart and a fourth of its young black men spent at least some of their lives in jail.

"Underfunded education is no accident," Jennifer said. "Society needs peons to wheel its loads and sweep its floors."

This got them all going, and they discussed capitalism over pumpkin pie. They drove to a party at a big house where candles in paper bags lined the driveway. A local rock band played on the lawn. Scott and Jennifer returned to their house ahead of the others, climbed the stairs and flung their room windows open. Curtains wafted in and out to the rustle of the sea. Scott braced a chair against the door and he and Jennifer slowly coupled.

Doors opened and closed, voices rose and fell on the terrace below. Scott slept and awoke, slept again. He dreamed it was night and he was lost in a big city. He could not find the right streets, he walked dangerous neighborhoods. It was a scary dream. He felt lost, abandoned. He could not remember where he lived.

He and Jennifer breakfasted in the morning amid sections of Sunday newspapers. They walked barefoot to the ocean and waded in the surf. Flat-bottomed clouds cast floating shadows and birds chased each other on the sand.

"I'm peopled out," Scott said. "It happens every Sunday when I do this beach house thing."

Jennifer shaded her eyes the better to look at him. "You should learn to relax," she said. "You don't need to try so hard."

CHAPTER 18

Scott Lehmann sat in the sun on the steps of the Federal Building and critiqued his performance as a guest at Jennifer Cohen's summer house. Better to try too hard than not try hard enough, he told himself.

Did he really want to share an apartment with Jennifer? Why did he suggest that anyway? It was probably her nearness, her swimsuit, a purple bird flying over.

What about skiing? Should he take her skiing this winter? Should they join a group house or stay in motels? What about inviting her to meet his parents in Illinois? He pictured his parents and her parents together. What would they talk about?

Scott bought a cup of tea and an apple raisin muffin and returned to his office. Barry Kalish stuck his head in. "There's a worthy new disco, young broker, Clutters on Albany Street. Next to the river, the other side of the new Trade Center."

"What should I wear?" Scott asked, half facetious.

"Something to excess. Don't hold back."

"Clutters, you say?"

"There's no sign outside. I'll tell you how to get there."

Friday night Scott wore what George Rogalski once called his "clown suit," bright stripes, flagrant tie, bell-bottom pants. He wondered for a moment, looking at himself in the mirror, "what is all this for? Where does it lead?" Jennifer Cohen's doorman did not recognize him.

She wore an off-shoulder black dress cleft high on one side. "Very nice, Jennifer." Scott kissed her neck. She glided across her rug and her stockinged legs whispered, "later, later."

"Wine?" she asked.

"We've got time."

They leaned on her terrace railing. The sun descended behind Jennifer's building and golden rays wandered down side streets and flung long shadows across roads in the Central Park. Runners puffed along down there, appearing, disappearing amid the trees.

They returned inside and Monet's *Houses of Parliament* held Scott's eye. Contrast struck him; the difference between Monet's murky London silhouettes and the clarity of Charles Russell's Montana prairies and mountains. Which did he prefer? Montana seemed the boldest answer, but tonight he felt stretched between.

Jennifer handed him a pink satin jacket. Scott held it and she backed into the sleeves and fastened it neatly in front with a bow.

They ate at a restaurant where the menu offered five "specials," all expensive, and waiters hovered at the edge of vision. "I like your suit," Jennifer said to Scott, apparently serious. He asked about her week at General Brands.

"Frozen chicken pot pies. You pop them in a microwave and peel an apple or something while steam puffs the package. You pour orange juice or make salad or call mom while heat browns the scrumptious morsels. A clever pad inside sops up the grease."

"You snap your fingers and little, metallic legs whisk it to your plate."

"Ha. Good idea."

They dined. They took a cab. Albany Street in lower Manhattan fronted apartments built on landfill bulldozed into the Hudson. Indeed, it appeared the architects sought to imitate the faded-brick feel of the City of Albany 130 miles north along the banks of this same river.

A tugboat chugged upstream. "Aren't you glad now you didn't dam the headwaters up there in the mountains?" Jennifer said.

Scott laughed, pleased that she remembered. He had not thought of that moment since their return from the Adirondacks.

Clutters awaited behind an unmarked door a level down from the street. The doorman looked at Jennifer in her pink jacket, lifted a rope and motioned them in. What about my suit? Scott tried to catch the gatekeeper's eye. Nothing.

They pushed through swinging doors as if into a gymnasium. Music thundered, people gyrated in fractured light. It was early, but the dance floor looked crowded.

Seats rose in widening circles from the crowded floor toward the ceiling. They climbed halfway up, sat, ordered drinks. Music thundered, a record that Scott especially liked. He and Jennifer rushed down to the dance floor. She looked up at the rows of people looking down. "It's like skiing under the lift," she said.

She caught the beat in her high heels, Scott fought for space. Multiple elbows hemmed them in. Other couples adapted to the crush by dancing nearly in place. It bothered Scott that they so readily accepted this restriction.

He and Jennifer climbed to their seats, swallowed half a drink, descended, danced again. Scott realized that he began to have fun.

A warm breeze lazed across the Hudson from New Jersey when finally they stepped outside. Scott waved for a cab. Jennifer walked a crack in the street, raised her arms for balance.

"Evening, Miss Cohen," her doorman said, his face noncommittal. The ascending elevator made no sound at all.

She flipped off her pink jacket, dipped as a ballerina might before her bedroom mirror and stepped out of her dress. Scott saw that she wore a garter belt with black stockings instead of her usual pantyhose. He had asked her earlier in the week to try this and then had forgotten about it. He picked her up and carried her into the bedroom.

He dropped her on the bed. "Make my nipples hard," she said. He stroked her. He kissed her little nodules.

"Make me spread my legs." She made a show of resisting, so he planted his knees and nudged her legs outward toward a V. Her ribcage strained. She squirmed. She seemed to look through and beyond him.

"Make me come." The garter belt and stockings proved no hindrance at all.

Mist shrouded Central Park in the morning. They ate cereal and toast and sat, toes touching. "Go for a run?" Scott suggested.

"I'm ready."

They jogged across Central Park West, through an opening in a stone wall and ran along a paved road under leafy trees north to a lake-like reservoir where hundreds of runners circled the water all going the same direction, clockwise.

They joined in. Twice they passed a fortress on the south side of the reservoir where runners sat, talked and stretched at stone portals. Moisture coated Scott's skin. Mist hung over the reservoir and hid the buildings that rose like amphitheater walls on either side of the park. "You live so close," he said to Jennifer, "you could do this all the time."

"I know."

They trotted back toward her apartment, Jennifer's ponytail bouncing with each stride. Scott, sweaty, loose, felt himself a member of a bold elite. He detected similar conceits in the eyes of other runners. There is an arrogance to feeling fit.

He sang in the shower an old Hank Williams song remembered from some lost tavern in the night. "...Tonight my head is bowed in sorrow. I can't keep the tears from my eyes. My son calls another man daddy; the right to his love I've been denied..."

Jennifer stepped in beside him. "You've known pain, haven't you, tall stranger?" They lathered each other amid splash and steam.

Scott glanced out her bathroom window. "Sun's trying to break through. We should take advantage."

They changed to jeans and t-shirts and strode west along Seventy-Second Street. A grassy park extended along Riverside Drive and they sat on a bench overlooking the Hudson River. North the George Washington Bridge vibrated with multiple layers of traffic. Cars swooshed past on Riverside Drive. Yells sounded from a basketball game, where blacks and Puerto Ricans sprinted back and forth on a concrete court.

"Tempted?" Jennifer asked.

"Maybe if Brent was here."

They sat talking, lazing in the sun. Returning to her place, they passed a video store. "Let me surprise you," Scott said.

"Oh sure, some god forsaken cowboy opus."

He found what he wanted. They sat on the terrace of her apartment tipping glasses of wine. Pockets of mist hovered in Central Park and horse-drawn hansoms clopped under the trees. Across the park, up and down Fifth Avenue, today's setting sun slowly climbed building walls. Windows flashed, flamed, darkened.

They walked to an Upper West Side restaurant and played at holding hands. It was a warm night, but they liked it when their waitress lit a candle on their outdoor table.

They strolled in summer darkness down Central Park West and sat on her couch to watch three horsemen meet on an endless prairie and ride toward a railroad station dot on the vast. "Do not forsake me, oh my darling," Tex Ritter sang on the movie soundtrack.

Gary Cooper, as Sheriff Will Kane, waits in a dusty town against the advice of his bride Grace Kelly, still in her wedding dress, against the advice of just about everyone, for a psychopath he has sent to prison and who has sworn to kill him to return on the noon train.

"Why don't you run?" his deputy sheriff asks.

"If you don't know," Gary Cooper says, "I can't tell you."

The bad man's three friends drink whiskey at the railroad tracks, waiting. Gary Cooper seeks help from the townspeople, but one by one they desert him. "It's all for nothing, Will," the gnarled, white- haired former sheriff says. "It's all for nothing."

A train whistles: high noon. Four gunmen stride an empty street and Gary Cooper, his seamed face a map of lost illusions, walks alone to meet them. He dodges from building to building, shoots one man, then another. Grace Kelly, his Quaker bride, who had planned to leave on the train, runs back and shoots a third in the back.

Gary Cooper and the psychopath killer face each other on a dusty street. Gary Cooper wins. The townspeople rush from hiding but Cooper does not speak to them. He looks around at this street, at this town, that he will never visit again. Slowly he removes his sheriff's badge from his shirt and drops it in the dust.

"I'd watch this movie just to see him do that," Scott said.

"Next time l choose the movie," Jennifer said.

"You liked it, though?"

"Gary Cooper possesses a certain, ragged dignity. What's the name of that town of your's in Illinois?"

"Grange."

"Grange." She rolled the word. "Perfect."

In bed, they played their game where she sits on him and tries to hold him down. "You're trapped, there's no way you can get out of this."

He shrugged her off like a cat flung from a pillow. "Oohh." He knew it excited her, this turning of the tables.

"Got you now." He held her down. Her lips thickened, her eyes darkened.

Central Park looked muddy and lost Sunday morning. A person in a yellow slicker walked a dog. They sat in bed with mugs of coffee and sticky moistness blew in the window. Jennifer padded to the kitchen and returned with cinnamon toast. "Your turn to go for the Sunday paper," she said.

They went for a run later. Scott expected, when he looked out and saw rain, to feel restless. But he did not. He glanced at muddy, stringy-haired Jennifer loping along beside him. "Do you see what's happening here?"

"What?" she asked.

"We're developing mutual interests."

CHAPTER 19

Monica Corbin balanced on one high heel holding a pile of envelopes from Manhattanites who responded to a recent Scott Lehmann mass mailing. He offered, to those who replied, a free booklet explaining the intricacies of tax-free municipal bonds.

"Not a bad response," Scott said. "You don't expect more than two or three to a hundred." He ought to ask Monica out for a drink, he thought. He visualized the two of them, heads together; he, the cunning veteran scattering nuggets of wisdom, she impressed, quick with questions. If the Golden Falcon, could play this role, so, by god, could he...

"I'll have the notes ready for you before you leave." Monica typed these individually, rather than run them off on a duplicating machine. Each stated that Scott Lehmann hoped the enclosed booklet proved helpful, and that he would soon follow with a phone call.

"No rush," he said. "Tomorrow's fine."

Within an hour she presented him a stack of neatly typed notes to sign. Scott smiled, feigned amazement. He would speak to Walter Cappaletti about giving her a raise, he decided. He would say afterward to Monica, "Oh, by the way, I talked to Walter..."

He put his feet up and gazed out his window. A heat wave oppressed New York and the stock market stagnated in late summer doldrums. Well, if his customers did not call, he would call them. He searched his account books, jotted names of clients sitting on worthy profits, and called them one by one. "Cameron, that computer stock we bought in January is up thirty per cent. But a profit is not actually a profit until you take it..."

Between calls his telephone rang. "Scott, Mr. Polinsky."

He flipped to the proper page in his account books. "You're sitting on some decent gains here, Mr. Polinsky. Now might be a good time..."

"I know, Scott, you may be right, but I'd like to buy an airline stock. Does your analyst have a favorite?"

Not surprisingly, the analyst did. Scott earned another commission.

He worked the telephone all afternoon and when the market closed calculated his income for the day. Not bad, but he needed to score high to maintain his standing as a Big Producer. He thought of George Rogalski toiling here at this desk to feed his family.

Scott stayed after Barry and Monica left, addressing envelopes for another mass mailing. He would meet Brent Hall and Ruth, the speech therapist, for dinner, so at six o'clock he slung his seersucker suit jacket over his shoulder, descended to Broadway and boarded a northbound subway. The train clacked along and he replayed today's conversation with Mr. Polinsky.

Scott had never met the man in person. He knew that Mr. Polinsky opened his hardware store twelve hours a day, six days a week and that he spoke briefly and to the point on the telephone. He imagined a man in his forties, not fat, no illusions, good at numbers. He had a business to maintain, a family to feed, and probably a monthly mortgage payment to meet. Mr. Polinsky should be advising him, Scott thought, not the other way around.

He climbed the stairs to Twenty-Third Street and walked to a restaurant on Lexington Avenue. Brent beckoned from a table. "Ruth," he said to a handsome woman in a red business suit, "meet Scott Lehmann, one of the keenest financial minds of our generation."

Ruth Challender's brown hair tumbled to wide, sturdy shoulders. She looked urbanely polished, in contrast to Brent's hollow-cheeked Oklahoma redness. A white handkerchief protruded from the chest pocket of her double-breasted jacket.

"I'll try to enunciate," Scott, ever the wit, said to the speech therapist. She chuckled in acknowledgement. Brent beamed.

Scott looked from Brent to Ruth and back again. Why does this work? he wondered. He often pondered this when he saw couples who seemed happy together.

"Hamptons?" he asked Ruth. "Fire Island?"

"I prefer the city on summer weekends. There's nobody here. You can get tickets to whatever you want."

"Scott's in a summer house at Davis Park. Jennifer's at Amagansett," Brent explained.

"I know Brent told you about our basketball games," Scott said. "Pull him out of bed at three in the morning, hand him a ball and he'll hit ten shots in a row."

"I've heard the stories. Now if he can carry some of those moves over to business publishing."

Business publishing? Scott looked to Brent, the textbook editor, for an explanation.

"I interviewed at *Business World* today," his friend said. "They want a Northeast Regional editor. I live in the Northeast; I know the business."

"You don't want to edit textbooks anymore?"

"I want to write a column for the *New York Times*. I want to announce Monday night football on television. But a step at a time, my friend, a step at a time."

Brent grinned at Ruth. It's for her, thought Scott. Country boy meets city girl; two and two make five.

Jennifer Cohen walked through the restaurant door. She wore her shiny black shoes, white blouse and short, dark skirt.

Ruth jumped up. "THAT Jennifer Cohen!" she said.

The two women had summered together as twelve-year-olds at a camp in the Catskills. They flung out names. "Do you remember...?" Ruth had grown up in Queens and resided these days on the Manhattan's Upper East Side.

"How did you and Jennifer meet?" she asked Scott. "How long have you lived in the city?"

"We met this summer. I've lived here three years, Eighth Avenue and Twentieth."

"Brent tells me you're from the Midwest. The city suits you?"

"It does. But I like to get away on weekends."

"I like the city too, but I don't see the it as an ideal place to bring up kids." Like most New Yorkers, when she said "the city," she meant Manhattan. Singlehood in Manhattan, she suggested, parenthood in the suburbs.

Scott watched Brent as she spoke and noted that he nodded once or twice and scratched his forehead.

"Speaking of quiet greatness," – Scott touched Jennifer on the shoulder – "this one climbed Mount Marcy."

"Biggest mountain in New York State," Jennifer explained. "A voice called Scott's name in the night."

"That's right," Scott said, a little embarrassed. "So I crawl out of the tent and that's when I see the Northern Lights."

"Brent waited two weeks after we met to call me," Ruth said.

"I was intimidated by her beauty," Brent said.

"I hope you two will come as our guests to Davis Park," Scott suggested, noting, as he did that Jennifer glanced at him bemused. He realized that with his "our" he incorporated her into his summer house's happy gang.

"You've heard of the Sixish?" Jennifer asked.

"It's a cocktail party on the sand, as I've heard Scott describe it," Brent said.

"'It's a meat market,'" Jennifer laughed and quoted Marlene Miller.

It was Wednesday night and the workday world awaited them tomorrow. They lingered on the sidewalk outside before separating. "Let's do this again," Brent said.

"Yes."

"Soon."

"Think about guesting at Davis Park," Scott said. "I mean it."

"We will, we will." Brent and Ruth walked down Lexington Avenue and turned west at the corner. "I think she's staying over at his place," Scott said.

"I like her," Jennifer said. "She's got the nerve to wear shoulder pads. She's wary of you, though. Did you sense that? I think she sees you as the bachelor friend to be won over."

"It pleases me that Brent likes you."

"You think so?"

"Oh yes. He cast some appreciative glances."

"We could do something together in the city, the four of us," Jennifer said, "but I don't think they are interested in a group expedition to Davis Park."

"Want to come out again this weekend?" Scott asked.

"You could join me in Amagansett. I spoke to Howard and he said there's room."

"Maybe we could do something different," Scott said. Interesting, he thought: apparently now they both assumed they would spend weekends together.

"You think and I'll think and we'll talk tomorrow."

"Yes," Scott said. He waved down a taxi for her and walked crosstown to his apartment.

Jennifer telephoned an hour later. "My father invites us to his place this weekend. Connecticut, overlooking Long Island Sound. It's about an hour drive from the city and he wants to take us sailing."

"Who else?"

"Just Dad and his new wife. Not so new: his second wife, I should say."

"All in the same wing of the manor?"

"Not to worry. Madeline will probably put us in a room together. Toss in a swim suit and tennis racket. Dad will probably want to take us to dinner at his club, so you should bring a sports jacket."

CHAPTER 20

A lawn sloped from the house to the shore of Long Island Sound and a gazebo shone on this expanse of green, a gazebo so white in the fading light that it looked freshly coated with snow. "Institutional?" asked Doctor Michael Cohen.

"Retail," Scott Lehmann said. "I have a few pension accounts but most of my accounts are individuals."

"How did you find them?" Madeline Cohen asked.

"Mass mailings. Telephone. I prospect mostly high income areas of uptown Manhattan."

"He possesses the metropolitan area's finest telephone voice," Jennifer Cohen said.

"Lucky you. Wall Street is selling," Dr. Cohen said. Scott expected dapper elegance, and faced instead a tall, brawny man with reddish hair beginning to thin. He expected a young blonde as new wife and faced instead an ample, fortyish brunette.

"How did you two meet? Madeline asked. Busty, tanned to the point of combustion, she looked in pants and backless high heels a motorcycle mama ready to ride.

"I tried to recruit him for another brokerage firm," Jennifer said. "Instead he recruited me."

"How so?" The father regarded Scott.

"He took me to a baseball game. He took me camping in the Adirondacks."

Madeline studied Scott. "He didn't kidnap you or something like that?"

Jennifer played with her arms. She wore a white jumpsuit and she knew she looked good. "I wanted to go," she said. "I wanted to see if I could do it."

They sat in the gazebo holding glasses of gin and tonic. Sails glided across Long Island Sound beyond the sloping lawn. The underwater lights of a swimming pool glowed.

"Mountain climbing seems to suit you, Jen," her father said.

"Once a year would be about right," she said. "You'd think in the Adirondacks you could put a tent up almost anywhere? Wrong."

"All we needed was a level few feet," Scott said. "Rocks and roots. Rocks and roots. We finally found a spot along a stream."

Madeline laughed and touched Jennifer on the knee. "I remember when you thought eating at a cafeteria was roughing it."

"Madeline and I looked at land in the Adirondacks," Dr. Cohen said. "Thought we might buy. Thought we might wait and subdivide when they changed the zoning. But politics, you know."

Scott knew. He liked it that conservationists worked to save the Adirondacks from development. "Used to be a sea of stumps up there," he said. "It was totally over logged sixty, seventy years ago. It was a wasteland. Then they made it a state park."

"They kicked a lot of people out of their homes to do it," the doctor said. "Regretfully, the world still needs trees to make paper, the kind you brokers write your buy and sell orders on, the kind we doctors use to write prescriptions, so somebody has to cut trees somewhere. But I'm not a total capitalist fart. I like parks. I like conservation."

Madeline looked gleefully at her husband. "Yes, you are, you are a capitalist fart." She leaped up. "Anybody hungry?"

Dr. Cohen walked Scott through his exercise room while Jennifer helped Madeline serve dinner. He had kilos and kilos of equipment and Scott tried several of the machines, pushing enough weight so that the doctor could see he knew what he was doing.

He had offices in Connecticut and New York City, Dr. Cohen said, and he specialized in sports related injuries. "Jennifer probably told you internal medicine. Right? That sounds more Park Avenue, but sports is where it's at today. So tell me. What's going to happen in the stock market?"

"Nixon will win in November. But we've had most of that rally already. Long term the market beats inflation."

"You have to like these computer stocks," the doctor said.

"I should pay more attention to computer companies. We've got analysts who visit companies, poke under tables."

"It's like medicine, you want specialists," the doctor said.

They dined on cold shrimp, corn on the cob, salad and apple pie.

Madeline turned to Scott. "Did he ask you about computers?"

"He did mention them, yes. But," Scott looked at Jennifer, "some astute people see packaging as the wave of the future."

"Thank you, Scott," Jennifer said. She proceeded to tell her father and Madeline all about her new job at General Brands.

The doctor assembled a host of after-dinner liqueurs and mentioned the sweeter and heavier ones first. He spoke reverently, in conclusion, of his apparent pride, an old, old cognac.

"I'd like to try that," Scott said. The doctor poured a small amount in a snifter and watched as gently – not too long, not too obvious – the younger man inhaled the aroma.

Scott sipped. He nodded. Jennifer snorted. "He likes it!" She burst into a smile.

The four of them strolled down the lawn to the water after dinner. A white sail glided silently across the darkness of Long Island Sound. "Where is it going?" the doctor asked. "Don't you wonder?"

"Hoboken," Madeline said. She told risque stories about their neighbors. They walked back up to the house and sat and talked in big chairs set up around a white table on the terrace.

Later the doctor said good night and Madeline led Scott and Jennifer upstairs. The three of them paused in the chill of air conditioning. "Here we are. You too, Scott." Madeline motioned them both in. He saw only one bed.

The lady of the house turned to leave. "Be good," she said.

"Her idea, dad's, I don't know." Jennifer laid away her jumpsuit and donned a peppermint nightie.

"You guested here with men before?"

"I'm thinking, I'm thinking...twice, yes – no, it wasn't Howard – a guy I thought I was serious about. I'm grown, you know."

"I'm picturing me bringing you home for a weekend to mom's or dad's in Grange, Illinois. They'd put us at opposite ends of the house with snarling guard dogs between."

"You think so?" Jennifer's hair riffed across her forehead. "They might surprise you."

"I doubt it. Maybe if we were ten years married."

"Madeline asked me what you were like. I said you had the patience of a plinth."

"A plinth?"

"Yes."

"What's a plinth?"

"I don't know. Something that doesn't have a lot of patience."

"Next time Madeline asks you, tell her all I want is to live happily ever after."

"That's not enough," Jennifer said. "You have to have an angle."

Scott sat on the bed beside her. "Look what I've got here."

"What?"

"A throbbing purple plinth."

Jennifer looked, and actually appeared to blush. They tried to couple quietly, no shenanigans.

It took over an hour in the morning to fit masts, unfurl canvas, to do all the things necessary to prepare a sailboat that Scott had never done before. Dr. Cohen started the engine – Scott didn't know that sailboats had engines – and they chugged out onto Long Island Sound in search of a breeze.

A puff. Another. "Let's ride this one," the doctor said. He cut the engine. Nothing happened. Then a sail filled, wood creaked, the boat gathered speed.

Jennifer dipped her hand in the wake. Scott shaded his eyes from the glint of the sun – he had forgotten to bring sun glasses – and observed how the doctor manipulated the rudder to steer the boat.

"Use these." The doctor produced an extra pair of dark glasses.

Scott put them on. He calculated sail angles. He studied horizons.

Bright sails speckled the water, patterned in many shades and hues.

"Look, there's two sails alike. See, they're drawn to each other," Jennifer said.

"Wine in earthen jars," Scott said. "Pressed olive oil and corn from Carthage bound for Messina."

Dr. Cohen smiled. "They get weather in the Mediterranean," he said. "Here the good winds don't blow until fall. I hate to miss a weekend. Sometimes in September, when there's a moon, we run all night to Newport."

Scott imagined running all night to Newport. "Storms could come up," he said.

"Sure. Lots of things could happen."

"I thought we'd be climbing masts, hauling jibs, stuff like that."

"You'd enjoy that, huh? Here, take the rudder for a while."

Scott grasped the wooden tiller and felt the push and shove of the wind. Coming about – changing directions – required practice, and the doctor showed him how to turn the rudder and duck his head as the sail shifted. The older man offered suggestions while Scott at the tiller steered a zigzag course across the Sound to a sheltered cove on Long Island.

"Here. Swing it sharp." The doctor flung out an iron anchor. He tossed two inflated air mattresses out on the water and hung a rope ladder from the side. He climbed to the railing and kerplunk! jumped overboard. "Come on," he yelled.

Scott and Jennifer jumped in and splashed about in the salty water. Bronzed Madeline, glistening with unguents, stretched in the sun on the deck of the boat.

Jennifer swam to one of the floating mattresses, crawled on top and lay on her tummy. So, Scott thought, that's what they're for. At the doctor's suggestion, he squirmed up on the other mattress, lay on his back and gazed up at a hazy, August sky.

"Come on in," Jennifer yelled to Madeline.

Madeline stirred, lifted a lazy hand and remained where she was.

"Better she stay there," Dr. Cohen said. "You don't want everybody in the water at the same time if an anchor tears lose or something."

After a while the three swimmers pulled themselves up the little ladder to get back on board. This was tougher than it looked, Scott discovered. His toes stubbed against the boat when he fixed his feet in the rope rungs and he had to grab tight to the railing above to hoist himself.

Madeline brought out cheese and little slices of fruit and offered cold beers around.

The doctor briefly started the engine to nudge them out into the wind for the sail home. Jennifer took the tiller, a baseball cap pulled low over her forehead. She steered back to Connecticut across Long Island Sound.

The Cohens leaped to action the instant they docked. Scott, a novice amid this flurry of movement, watched and tried to help. Openings needed to be sealed, sails folded, everything stored away again.

They rode to land in a little putt-putt and walked up the hill toward the house. Jennifer suggested tennis and to Scott's surprise the older couple agreed. They changed clothes, hopped a hedge to a neighbor's court, and the four of them played doubles.

Jennifer raced about, white panties peeking, drops of perspiration glistening on her upper lip. Madeline and the doctor hit hard and served well. Scott at least did not embarrass himself. He enjoyed almost any game – except golf or squash – that involved a ball.

The men relaxed with drinks on the terrace while the women showered. "What are your plans?" the doctor asked. "Do you hope to advance to management?"

Scott started to make his usual reply, that he liked it where he was, but decided to tack with the wind. "We'll see," he said. "I enjoy what I do now, but that might change."

"You never know," the older man said.

"I keep thinking of you running with the moon to Newport," Scott said. He imagined dark shores, sails straining. He couldn't get it out of his mind.

"Next time we'll take you along."

"I wasn't angling for that."

"But you'd enjoy it?"

"Sure, moon, smell of fall coming: I think it would be an adventure."

Jennifer approached down a flagstone path in a black dress with tiny shoulder straps, jingly bracelets and her usual shiny, low-heeled shoes. Dr. Cohen flashed Scott a contemplative, questioning look. "I'll go see if there's any hot water left," he said.

"Are you getting along with Dad?" Jennifer asked.

"I think so."

"He offered you his old cognac last night; that's a good sign."

They drove to a yacht club and dined on an outdoor balcony. Sailboats bobbed on the water below. "This is the way I picture hilltop villages above the Mediterranean," Scott said.

Why did he say that? Now he had to explain that, no, he had not visited hilltop villages in Europe. He danced a slow one with Madeline. "What religion are you?" she asked.

"I was raised a Lutheran."

"Which is the one where they tilt you in the water?"

"That's the Baptists, I think."

"When you go to heaven, do you become younger, or do you have to stay at the age you were when you died?"

"I don't know," Scott said. "I'm an atheist myself."

"I wouldn't like spending my days with those who have gone before. I'd go batty with boredom."

Jennifer danced with Scott. "Did Madeline ask you about religion?"

Later, in their room, she asked him to undo her dress and slide it slowly down her back. She peeked at Scott over her shoulder. "Hilltop villages? Give me a break," she said.

They breakfasted on the patio in the morning, overlooking the water. "I never tire of this view," Jennifer said.

"I worried we might take it for granted, but I don't think we do," Madeline said. "At least I don't," she added, with a glance at her husband.

"It's nice," Dr. Cohen said, "as long as we can afford the upkeep. Speaking of," he glanced at Scott, "I'm always interested in new investment ideas. Why don't you give me a call next week."

CHAPTER 21

"Barry, why do the dogs run so fast in South Dakota?"

"Why?"

"Because the trees are so far apart." Scott Lehmann slapped his thigh. It was Monday morning.

Barry Kalish leaned against the wall of his office. Scott had grown used to seeing Barry haggard on Mondays, but it seemed that this morning he looked especially ravaged. "You'd better get some sleep, old timer," Scott said.

"There's a new discotheque," Barry said. "The Souffle."

"Is that the one in the airplane hangar?"

"No, this is the one where the mattress factory used to be."

"I meant to tell you; I took Jennifer to Clutters."

"Oh yeah. That place still around?"

The market opened lower. Scott gazed out his window. It was cooler today and the wind blew from the north out of a streaked, autumn-like sky. The new World Trade Center towers sparked in the sun.

The market opened lower and Scott stuck his head into Barry's office. "You're looking good on the oils." Barry recently sold several oil stocks short, on the theory that overproduction would drive prices down, and this morning stocks in that group did indeed decline.

But as Scott and Barry watched, the moving yellow-green numbers seemed to pause and consider. The selling slowed, the wind shifted, the market began to turn. One oil stock up ticked, another, and the market began to climb.

Up and down Wall Street, across Europe, in Japan, others watched their terminals and noticed the change. Sellers in Frankfort thought, "I'll wait," and pulled back offered stock. Buyers in Hong Kong thought, "Now," and reached for their phones.

"I don't like this," Barry said. "What would George say?"

"'Don't fight the trend.'"

"Too late, I done fought it," Barry said. The market continued to climb and Scott heard laughter. He glanced out at the rows of cubicles and saw two of the younger brokers slap palms. Satisfaction reigned out there. Be fair, Scott told himself. He remembered from his freshman days how he tended to celebrate, to think himself a market wizard, when stocks he bought rose in price.

"I'm out. I covered my short sales," Barry said.

"Good," Scott said. Now he could enjoy this rally without guilt.

He sat in the sun later with Art Levin on the steps of the Federal Building. "Jennifer took me to Connecticut to meet her dad. We played tennis. We sailed across Long Island Sound."

"He must be an agile old geezer. What does he do?"

"He's a doctor. He's got a house on the water, a second wife, and he's looking for investment ideas."

Art lifted his arms in triumph. "Boldly ventured, rightly dared; celebrate, the prize is snared. Plaudits, Storm."

"He asked me to call him but I think I'll wait a day or two. I don't want to appear too eager."

"Call him. Call him quickly," Art said.

"You think?"

"Ten brokers want to prospect him this week, but he asked you."

"I know, but I'm dating his daughter."

"So?"

"I'll do it, I'll call this afternoon. Did you go out to our house last weekend?"

"Marlene Miller's got a new guy. Larry Silverman wanted to know if you broke up with Jennifer. Naturally he hoped that you had. I met someone at the Casino. She's from Iowa and she works at an art gallery."

"Where does she live?"

"Upper East Side. She's from Iowa, I told you."

"She lives by herself?"

"Two roomies. She guested at somebody's house at Davis Park."

"The thrill of the chase. Good luck, Lamont."

Scott bought a cup of tea and an apple-raisin muffin and shared an elevator with Monica Corbin and Bruce Stanton, who apparently had lunched together. A lipstick smear reddened Bruce's chin.

Stocks continued to climb. Jennifer's father had mentioned computers, so Scott searched through research reports, began a process of elimination and settled finally on two recommendations. He phoned Doctor Michael Cohen's office on the West Side near Columbus Circle.

"Scott, the doctor sees patients today. He asked me to tell you he would return your call tomorrow morning."

Good; Scott stalked about energized. He telephoned other customers, recommended the two computer stocks and wrote several buy orders. He telephoned Brent Hall and suggested basketball after work.

"Wish I could. Developments."

"You got the new job at *Business World*."

"Nope, that's still pending. Ruth and I intend to get married."

"Oh, Jesus." Scott visualized his basketball buddy disappearing into suburbia. "How did this happen?"

"I took her to dinner last night at the restaurant on Lexington Avenue where we met you and Jennifer. A woman at the next table began to cry because the guy she was with gave her a necklace. I asked Ruth to marry me."

"Did she hesitate, seem to consider?"

"No. We jumped straight to the details."

"So I guess you've been thinking about it then?"

"We had discussed it."

"Well, congratulations," Scott said.

"We'll do it soon and we'll invite a few friends," Brent said. "I don't have brothers and my father's dead. I'd like you to be my best man. Ruth and I will live in Manhattan for the time being and I still want to play basketball and discuss, over steamer clams, the great ideas."

"We can do that," Scott said.

The temperature had dropped since lunch hour and it felt cool for early September when he left his office. He rode the subway several stops north, decided he needed exercise, and exited at Houston Street to walk the remaining twenty-five blocks to his apartment on West Twentieth. A breeze blew from the north and the feel of fall in the air excited him.

Two men argued over a garbage can at Charles Street and Seventh Avenue. "Here," an old man in work shoes and undershirt yelled. "Always I put it here."

The second man, young, wore shorts and a polo shirt. "Idiot, you're not supposed to put it there." He wrestled the garbage can away and pushed it toward the curb.

"Now you've done it, you sonofabitch bastard," the old man said. "You go away from here."

"Larry," the young man called. "Larry. Come out here!"

"I'll kill you, you faggot."

"You old queen. Larry! Come out here."

He ought to write down some of this stuff, Scott thought. A rush hour tangle of cars and taxis choked Seventh Avenue, originally, according to legend, an Indian trail. Manhattan Island was probably a fine place to camp then, a green island between two silver rivers.

Crossing Fourteenth, Scott caught a glimpse of the Empire State Building and tried to imagine wild forest where the building now stood. He tried to visualize bears prowling about. It didn't work. It was concrete now, pure and simple. He got home, called Jennifer Cohen, and told her Brent's news.

"Is Ruth pregnant, do you think?"

"Hmmm. I don't think so."

"Well, I forecast this marriage will last. Did you call my dad?"

"He was out; his secretary said he'd get back to me tomorrow."

"He remembered. I told you he would."

"I bought those fish sticks you suggested. What do I do now?"

"Your microwave still working? Good..." Scott jotted directions. He heated frozen chunks and sliced a lemon. The fish tasted mushy, but it was healthy food, he told himself.

Jennifer's father called in the morning shortly after the market opened. "Scott, sorry I missed you yesterday." "You mentioned computer stocks."

"Our analyst has two favorites, Intergraphics and National Computer." Scott described them.

"You like them yourself?"

"I'm recommending them to other clients."

"Buy me ten thousand dollars worth of each. Round the purchases off in even hundreds of shares; it doesn't matter if you run a thousand or two over."

"I need to ask you some questions." Rather than enlist Monica's help, this time Scott filled out the new account form himself. Dr. Cohen stipulated Madeline, his second wife, as his beneficiary in the event of his death, and if Madeline also died he divided his estate between Jennifer and her sister.

"That's all you need? Good. Have your assistant phone me the amount due and I'll mail you a check this afternoon."

"Thank you, Doctor."

"Michael," the older man said. "Call me Michael."

CHAPTER 22

"Got time for coffee after work?" Scott Lehmann faced Monica Corbin, who today wore high heels, a leather skirt, a diaphanous purple blouse and lilac stockings. It was accepted at Tuttle, Osborn & Durkin, perhaps even encouraged, that the women sales assistants dress as street walkers. Not so, of course, the women brokers.

"Sure," Monica said. "What's on your mind?"

"Our futures. Our very destinies."

"Oh, only that." Monica smiled. She knew him now.

Scott sat at his desk and listened, as he did every day, to the morning call. Analysts took turns selling their wares. "...window of opportunity..." one of them said.

"I can't stand it." Scott groaned loud enough for Barry to hear.

Barry stuck his head in. "Which is worse," he asked, "'window of opportunity' or, 'at this point in time?'"

"Equally awful."

"The trick is to use them both in the same sentence."

The market opened. Scott glanced out at Monica. She flexed the calf muscle of a crossed leg and the high heel on her lifted foot slid on and off, on and off.

He worked his telephone. National Computer and Intergraphics traded actively, up an eighth or a quarter of a point, and he recommended both stocks to his customers. He wrote orders. He thrived on this feeling of functioning, of doing business.

A client who worked down the street popped in to talk. "What about inflation?" the man asked.

Scott stroked his chin. He heard, "What about inflation?" in his dreams. "We look at real estate as well as stocks and bonds," he said. "We want to hedge Armageddon, we put five per cent into gold." He clicked off other specific long-term recommendations. Traders provided lots of commissions but tended to burn themselves out. Scott had come to realize that conservative investors formed the bedrock of his business.

"I'll get back to you," the man said.

The Golden Falcon, Bruce Stanton, hovered near Monica's desk. Scott waited and stepped out after Bruce left. "I know I mentioned coffee after work," he said. "But if you've got the time, I'll take you to dinner."

Monica did not hesitate. "I'd like that," she said.

Scott had second thoughts: he was her boss, of course she had to say yes. She disappeared at a few minutes to five and when she returned he saw that she had added lipstick and tucked her blouse in tighter. He wondered if she also talked to Bruce. Though she sat just outside his door, he rang her on the telephone. "Ready?"

"Yes." She replied, without turning toward him.

They walked out side by side and Scott saw Bruce Stanton glance, look away, look again.

He suggested Marshmellow, a bar-restaurant he liked on East Fifty-Second Street. "Since you live in the West Eighties, it will be on your way home."

"Anything north of here is on my way home."

The sun slanted down the streets. Today, for some reason, Scott noticed buildings and people as if seeing everything new. He stared out from the back seat of a cab riding up Broadway. He saw stone gargoyles, hooded arches, storefronts he never noticed before.

The early Marshmellow crowd congregated along the bar and Scott chose a window table. He realized this was the first time in two months that he escorted a woman other than Jennifer Cohen.

Well, why not? He knew Jennifer enjoyed after-work libations with her packaging gang. "Martini?" he asked. Monica nodded. He ordered two.

"Somebody told me you did television commercials," she said.

"I did one for Lancer Hair Cream," Scott said, pleased that she knew. "Monica, you could be a model."

"I'd rather be a stockbroker. Regular paychecks. A nice desk."

Scott nodded professionally. "It's hard at first, but once you build your business..."

It pleased him, examining the menu, that he no longer paid much attention to prices. He felt for a moment the excitement of money as freedom, of freedom as money.

"I'll get to the point," he said. "I intend to ask Walter to pay you more. But first I wanted to talk to you. Any wishes? Any problems? What's your timetable for becoming a broker yourself?" She would see through this, of course. If she deserved a raise she should get one, but his rogue itch crystalized. He wanted to see how far he could go.

"I hope to take the test to qualify as a stockbroker as soon as I can, and I want to do it with our firm, not somebody else." Monica leaned in. "I spoke to Walter about a raise. He thinks the first of the year, but that's four months away; meanwhile I lost my roommate – she went back to Massachusetts – so now I pay my apartment rent alone. I discussed this with Barry. Did he tell you?"

"No," Scott said, surprised. "I was going to bring this up with him."

"I asked around the office," Monica said. "Most of the more established brokers, the one's with private offices like you and Barry, supplement their sales assistants' salaries themselves."

"You mentioned this to Barry? What did he say?"

"He offered to supplement my salary a hundred and fifty a month. He said he thought you might do the same."

"A hundred and fifty." Scott pondered. That was eighteen hundred dollars a year. "Remember, it's cash," he said. "It's tax free."

"Yes, thank goodness," Monica said.

"A hundred and fifty a month. I'll do it, starting October first."

"I appreciate that," she said.

Scott signaled for another round. "Monica, you're the best sales assistant I've had. I wanted to talk compensation with you and it embarrasses me to hear that you Walter and Barry beat me to it."

He remembered that she had gone to Bennington College, and he made a motion as if holding ski poles. "Did you ski up there in Vermont?"

"We demonstrated our independence at Bennington by not skiing. Actually I did try it once, at Prospect Mountain. I bet you're a good skier."

"I enjoy it," Scott said.

"Bruce Stanton is an expert, or so he says. He wants me to take lessons this winter."

"Bruce certainly has discovered our area of the office."

"I have to laugh sometimes," Monica said. "Barry calls him the Golden Falcon."

Should he tell her he had coined the phrase? Scott looked into Monica's eyes. Old instincts never die. It was time to roll the dice.

"Yes?" she said.

"Monica, do you like to dance?"

"I like to dance."

"There's a new disco, The Souffle. It's on West Fourteenth near the docks and I'm guessing it's not crowded in the middle of the week. We could give it a go after we eat. We might actually have room to dance."

"Remembering, of course, that it is a week night, and that tomorrow we must remain alert."

"Yes indeed," Scott said.

Their meals arrived. She asked where he had grown up and where he had gone to college. Scott asked her about Waycross, Georgia, expecting some horrific tale. It turned out she only spent two summers there, and that her father worked, until he died suddenly of a heart attack, as an auto executive in Michigan.

They rode a taxi toward the lighted windows of the financial district. Near the Hudson River, in a former factory on West Fourteenth Street, they entered a cavernous room. Music thundered. Monica strode out on the floor in her high heels, leather skirt and see-through blouse and began to dance.

It surprised Scott that at first she seemed a little tentative. He recalled the black baseball star who admitted he did not know how to dance and the amazement that had caused.

Scott had joked to Brent Hall that in movies and on television whites who wanted to prove their funkiness sprinkled blacks around. The white guy sings or dances, the black onlookers, skeptical at first, admire and begin to clap. Presto, the white slob's authenticated.

Maybe Monica had not danced that much in her particular past. She loosened, though, what with the drinks and the noise, and they stayed out on the floor more or less continuously for a long time.

They also downed a number of drinks. Scott fancied he heard the Hudson River gurgling a block or two away when finally they exited into the night. "I could show you my place," he said. "It's not far. We could walk."

"Not in these heels," she said. A cab pulled up. People got out. They got in.

"I don't want Barry to hear about this," Monica said.

"No."

"Nor Walter. No one."

"Promise," Scott said.

"I know I could say no, but I'm curious too," Monica said.

They could see the lighted dome of the Empire State Building from where they landed on his bed. Everything looked violet to Scott, her clothes, her eyes. He asked her to slide her high heels on again.

He escorted her downstairs at three in the morning and waited until a cab stopped.

Scott arrived before she did at the office in the morning and it seemed to him that Bruce Stanton smiled faintly as he walked in.

"I talked to Monica," Scott said to Barry Kalish. "A hundred and fifty a month is fine with me."

"A hundred and fifty? That's what you decided?"

"I thought that's what you two decided," Scott said.

"A hundred, a hundred and fifty. We left it hanging."

"A hundred and fifty then," Scott said. "It won't go on and on.

She'll become a broker within a year."

Monica strode in briskly. "Morning, guys."

A week later she moved in with Bruce Stanton. As promised, Scott and Barry began to supplement her salary. She continued to perform her sales assistant tasks as if she had written the manual.

CHAPTER 23

Scott Lehmann and Jennifer Cohen took a taxi to Manhattan's East Side on a hot Saturday afternoon in September to see Brent Hall and Ruth Challender get married.

The ceremony was in a church. Jennifer wore a short, rosy dress and Scott rented a tuxedo. Brent said there would be a small crowd, mostly Ruth's family, and so it was. An usher led Jennifer to a seat while Scott poked through a labyrinth of hallways looking for his friend.

He found him alone in a small room seated on a folding metal chair. Sunlight from a high window streamed down on Brent's head and Scott stopped, caught by the scene. "The Last Supper," he said.

"What time is it?"

"Twenty minutes to kickoff."

"I've two relatives here, an aunt and an uncle from Oklahoma City. That's it." Brent looked especially skinny today.

"It's not the size of the crowd, it's the heart...how does that go?"

"The race is not to the swift," Brent said. "Time and chance happenth to us all." He was now Northeastern Regional Editor at *Business World* – Scott had seen his name on the masthead. He and Ruth had rented an apartment on East Sixty-Eighth Street and they planned to buy a car.

"Greatness lies in the undefinable." Scott quoted an adage Brent coined one night after basketball.

"Actually I feel pretty good about this. I'm ready. I was nervous, perhaps, throughout the planning. Now, let's get it done. We considered including a mass, but decided it would take too long."

A tap sounded on the door and a bearded man in black entered. "Father," Brent said, "this is Scott Lehmann, my best man."

"Lehman. Are you...?"

"Two Ns. No," Scott said. The priest led them down hallways and out into bright lights on a sort of stage. Scott saw a large room perhaps one-third filled with people. The priest prayed and Scott peeked and saw people cross themselves, something he always wondered about. The hand movements reminded him of sports rituals, of the habits athletes form.

The couple stood beneath an arbor of flowers and the ceremony moved briskly along. Brent and Ruth had collaborated on the words for the prayers and for the exchange of rings and vows, and Scott detected his friend's whimsical influence in the final editing.

His turn came to present the ring. The priest took it and slid it onto Ruth's finger. The priest introduced the new couple to the audience and everyone applauded. They all spilled outside into the sun. Taxis honked, pedestrians hurried past.

Scott glanced at his watch – two people from separate backgrounds, who did not even know each other a few months ago, had in about an hour presumably locked themselves together for life.

Ruth's father ran a paving contracting business in Queens and the Challenders rented a big, second-floor room in a restaurant on Central Park South for the reception. Flowers and little gifts for the guests dotted the tables. Scott made for the rows of champagne bottles and drained two quick glasses to Jennifer's one while Ruth and Brent worked the crowd.

A rock band began to play, the guitarist heavy on the low notes, the way Scott liked it. Mindful of his duty as a participant in the ceremony, he danced slower songs with the bridesmaids and the faster ones with Jennifer.

He approached the bride's mother, the tall and solid Mrs. Challender, and they danced cautiously about a foot apart.

"I've never been able to figure out my daughter's taste in men," she said. "I think she became a speech therapist to spite me."

"What did you want her to become?"

"A professor, a television personality; someone who talks instead of listens."

Scott laughed. He watched Jennifer pirouette across the room with yet another older man.

Brent wandered, red-faced, smiling at everyone. Ruth said softly to Scott, "You two keep on playing basketball. I think it's best we ease him into marriage."

"We'll try not to wear him out, though," Scott said.

He found other opportunities to speak with Brent before he and Ruth drove away. He danced with Jennifer and her hair swirled, her earrings swung. Between dances they drank champagne. "You're wearing your golden haze," Scott said.

They strolled in soft early evening along the southern boundary of Central Park. Trees rustled, sunset colors gentled the sky. "I really need to use your bathroom," Scott said.

He fidgeted as the elevator crawled up to her floor. He rushed down the hall, cursed the recalcitrant apartment door and made it just in time. He stepped out, relieved, and Jennifer stood quietly in the middle of her living room. She lifted her arms and he helped shake her rosy dress away.

They ran into the bedroom. Scott had not seen her for nearly a week and he needed, he wanted, to touch her all over, to know it all. Glancing down, he noted what seemed to him one of his more impressive erections. "Pearl," he said, "let's smuggle this one into town."

Next morning they sat up in bed with coffee and read the Sunday *Times*. Jennifer opened windows and padded about,

Scott turned pages. "The wedding's not in here." Ruth's parents said it would be.

"Too soon," Jennifer said.

"Who would marry us?" he asked.

"A reform rabbi. Orthodox and Conservative don't do mixed." She eyed him. "You really care about this?"

"I'm interested."

"The rabbi would pray in Hebrew and then in English. You would notice that God gets the credit, not Jesus."

"Doesn't somebody trample on a champagne glass?"

"You would," Jennifer said.

"Why would I?"

"In memory of the destruction of the Temple of Jerusalem. It's a suspenseful moment in the ceremony, everyone sighs, everyone says, 'Mazel Tov.' Some people stamp on light bulbs wrapped in cloth instead of champagne glasses because it's easier."

"June's the favored month?" Scott asked.

"The month doesn't matter if you're Jewish. The day might, though. Some consider Tuesdays lucky for weddings because Tuesday was the third day of creation, though if the truth be told I've never known anybody who actually got married on a Tuesday."

"Saturdays?"

"Some Orthodox frown on Saturday weddings before dusk. It's our Sabbath, you know."

"This is interesting," Scott said. He caught her look and added, "No, really."

"Another time-honored touch; in order to enhance consummation, some Jewish couples will not see each other for a week before the wedding. Morning or afternoon weddings are recommended, rather than night time, so neither party will go to bed overtired."

She waited. "What do you think of that?"

"Makes sense," Scott said. "I guess customs develop for a reason."

"Changes creep in," Jennifer said. "Many don't use kosher wine at the reception anymore, but if they do they decant it, because it's plebeian to pour from the bottle. It used to be that if the groom or bride were not Jewish, they had to attend an Introduction to Judaism class and affiliate with a congregation."

"Actually sign up, you mean?"

"Show your face now and then. Act like you care."

"That's not so bad."

"It's not required anymore. Interfaith marriages have become pretty common."

"What about the kids?" Scott asked.

"That can be a tussle, because you have to decide in which faith to raise them."

"How do you feel about that?"

Jennifer pursed her lips and looked afar, as if considering this for the first time. "Some couples expose their kids to both faiths and when they're old enough let them decide. It doesn't matter that much to me, actually."

"That's good."

"But..."

"But...?"

"I would not want them to grow up cut off from culture. I would like them to grow up in a city."

"Let me guess which city," Scott said.

CHAPTER 24

"What do you think Larry and the others will say when they find out I'm not going to Oregon?"

"They will be stunned. They will throw up their hands in amazement."

Art Levin had told members of their summer house that he intended to move to Eugene, Oregon, but yesterday New York University Law School accepted him. Today, he and Scott Lehmann cradled cups of Scotch and melted ice, dozing gulls shifted from foot to foot atop wooden pilings, and a ferry nudged them slowly out into Great South Bay.

Scott hoisted his drink toward a waning September sky. This weekend he and Jennifer Cohen separately bid farewell to their respective summer houses. Each had friends to hug and clothing and other possessions to claim.

"Lamont laughs, Lamont sings; he'll be ready when the bell rings," Art rhymed, loud enough for women nearby to overhear. "We've walked the raw edge of greatness, eh, Storm?"

"Indeed we have, Lamont Gramercy Cranston, indeed we have."

Scott studied sky and ocean. "How long does law school take?" he asked.

"Three years for most people," Art said. "Two years for me, I hope, because I will pile on credits and attend summer classes. I keep my apartment. I commute by subway."

"Finances?"

"Actually, I do have some savings, and I think my parents will contribute."

Darkness arrived much earlier now than it had in June and July and a last golden band of light hovered over Long Island. The gaslights of Davis Park flickered ahead across dark water. Scott and Art nodded at faces they knew. Some they might see next summer, some never again.

They landed and trod familiar wooden walks. Waves boomed beyond the dune. Scott saw their house ahead, glowing like an inflated paper dome.

Larry Silverman held down his usual seat at the bar. Marlene Miller glanced up from filing her nails and waved hello. Barbara Feldstein, immersed in a stack of test papers from her eighth grade English classes at Scarsdale, nodded from a corner.

Scott took in the smudged windows, the candles in Chianti bottles, the bleary furniture. He remembered his anticipation in May. Who would he meet? What would he learn?

Art poured a drink, cleared his throat. "Altered image, change of pace; I've staked my future on a different race." He related in detail the intricacies of his acceptance at N.Y.U.

"What kind of law will you specialize in?" Barbara asked. She seemed impressed.

"Corporate, estate; I don't know yet," Art said.

Marlene had ordered sandwiches from the mainland and these arrived. They sat around chewing, drinking juice, wine. Barbara ate and returned to her stack of papers. Scott sat next to her. "Tests already?" he asked.

"Grammar," Barbara said. "That's how we begin each semester. I can do these fast. Essays require subjective judgements. I'll ask that from them later on."

"You assign books for them to read?"

"The usual. *Huckleberry Finn. To Kill A Mockingbird.*"

"You live on East Eighty-Fifth, right? You drive to Scarsdale every day? How long does that take?"

"In my little Volkswagon thirty minutes maybe."

"You come home, park on the street in the city?"

Barbara smiled. "It's not bad," she said.

"Why don't you come with us to the Casino tonight?"

"Maybe later. You guys go on."

A man in a red blazer came for Marlene. Scott, Art and Larry clattered away on a wooden walk. Already it grew chilly. Stars crowded the sky and the ocean beyond the dune made long, cracking sounds.

"Rachael out this weekend?" Art asked Larry Silverman.

"I'll see her at the Casino," Larry said.

He had met Rachael, the daughter of a Chinese doctor, at a commercial shoot for his ad agency. She represented the client, an apartment store chain. "She's Chinese, and she's named Rachael?" Scott had asked him.

"Her mother's Jewish," Larry said.

The three men climbed wooden stairs to a quieter, more contemplative Casino. The music did not sound, or the place appear as crowded, as Scott tonight wanted it to be.

Willowy Rachael awaited. She and Larry danced. Art talked football, the New York Giants, with two guys along the bar. Scott hid his gin and tonics behind the jukebox and danced with different women but he missed Jennifer Cohen. He wondered what she did at Amagansett and with whom.

To his surprise, Barbara Feldstein walked in. She wore a blue sweater and snug pants and a new pair of glasses, smaller, that did not make her eyes look huge. Scott happened to be standing near the door when she entered. "Well," he said.

"Hello, Scott."

"Important question," he said, "you told me you had about a hundred students in four classes. How long does it take you to remember all their names?"

She looked at him with sort of a smile. "A week maybe," she said. A slow song played on the jukebox. Art Levin saw her and came over and asked her to dance.

Scott did not ask new women for phone numbers tonight. He danced, talked with people he knew and decided around eleven thirty to stroll home along the beach. Waves thundered in.

He passed a lifeguard stand so he climbed up to the seat and sat facing the ocean. The waves made long cracking sounds. Scott thought back over his summer. Actually, it seemed like two summers now, one before he met Jennifer Cohen, another after, with a parenthesis close to the middle, his night with Monica Corbin.

He climbed down after a while, crossed the dune on wooden stairs and approached his house. Art Levin and Barbara Feldstein sat on the deck and Barbara rose as he approached. "Good night, you two," she said. "I"m going to bed."

"She looked good tonight, huh," Scott said.

"Yes, I must admit. You assembled your thoughts on the beach, Lash Storm?"

"Poignant thoughts, Lamont; the rush of time, the realization of another season gone."

"I suppose you wonder why I applied to law school in New York rather than at the University of Oregon."

"I do," Scott said, "and I'm expecting you to tell me."

"My parents."

"Yes?"

"They're old, Storm."

They sat silent. Scott thought he knew what his friend meant.

A lowering sky greeted them Saturday morning, rents of blue scudding on the wind. The wind tore the tips from breaking waves and flung foam along the beach. The three men lobbed a football around, hoping for competition to arrive, but no other players appeared.

Art wore his jersey with the big number 88 on the back. "It's ten years from now," Scott said. "It's Old Timers Day. A crowd of ninety thousand roars in anticipation."

Larry guessed Scott's intention. "Gathered to honor one man. Gathered for one last, heroic moment."

"A nation grieves, a victory-stained jersey says farewell today." Scott and Larry turned toward Art, who trotted across the sand holding the football.

"There he is!"

"He's running out on the field!"

Art stopped, bowed to an imaginary throng.

"Hear the crowd! My god!"

"They rise, they cheer!"

The sun emerged but felt without heat. Left-handed Larry had a strong arm and Scott and Art took turns racing along the hard sand close to the water, seeing how far Larry could throw. They wore swimsuits and sweat shirts and finally all three shucked the shirts and ran into the ocean just so they could say they did it. They lasted about a minute.

The beach never did get crowded. Clouds trundled in again, from the east this time. They walked back toward the house around three o'clock. "It may be the last time I tread this wooden walk," Scott said.

"It may be the last time I touch this doorknob," Art said when they reached the house.

"Well done today, guys," Larry said. "It may be the last time I will compliment you."

Around five, preparing for the sixish, Scott poured a quart of gin into the blue enamel coffee pot. A sudden flash of sun lit the house. "God wants this sixish," Marlene Miller said.

"Barbara, come with us," Larry said.

"I don't know." She wore a tattered librarian's sweater.

"Come on, Barbara, fling yourself out there," Larry said.

The men changed to their talk-to-women attire. Barbara and Marlene Miller climbed the stairs arm in arm. Each wore crimson lipstick and a snug blouse. The five of them set forth, a daisy chain of color on a gray wooden walk, and approached the hallowed square of sand.

It was not nearly as crowded as during the summer but zest hovered in the air, even nostalgia. Scott, managing the coffeepot, made sure to keep Barbara's glass filled. At one point the two stood on the sand away from the others. "Take off your spectacles," Scott suggested.

"I can't see."

"Try it. We'll all be dead some day."

Barbara swept off her glasses, the same smaller pair she had worn last night, and stared at him, a freckle or two newly evident, a tartness, an appealing availability.

Scott peered into her eyes. "I thought so: a lusty, smoldering brown."

"And now?" Barbara put her glasses back on.

"Leave them off. You can see to walk, can't you?"

Larry Silverman, talking nearby with the willowy Rachael, took in the situation. "I'll hold your glasses for you, Barbara. I'll keep them in my protective pouch." He slid them into his fanny pack, where he carried dried beef jerky, god knows what.

Rachael, sleek and slim, smiled at Scott's blue enamel pot. "Coffee, yes," she kidded. "We'll all need some later, I'm sure."

Scott wandered the edge of the crowd, not ready for this last Sixish of summer to end. Barbara Feldstein extended her glass to be filled. Scott tipped the coffee pot, shook it, and discovered it nearly empty.

"Drat," Barbara said.

Scott instinctively bent and kissed her. "Barbara, I think you're the most intelligent, the most balanced, of us all."

She looked at him. "Well thank you, Scott." They stood quietly, looking out to sea. Night descended and Scott had not even noticed. Birds swooped, people stood in clusters, lingering. Larry approached and on impulse kissed Barbara too.

Almost dark now. Rachael left with her crowd. Marlene joined them and the five housemates clumped along a wooden walk and clustered on the deck of their weekend home. "End-of-the-summer ceremony," Art suggested.

"Yes, something official," Marlene Miller said.

They collected driftwood and Scott ignited a crackling blaze on the sand. He ran inside to get his blue bathing suit and held it above the flames. "Old Blue, go on through," he repeated three times and dropped his swimsuit into the fire to be consumed.

Others offered sacrifices. Someone produced a large bottle of wine. They intended to prepare supper, but Marlene knew of a party at a big house near the ocean. Barbara, floating now, deposited her spectacles in her room and came along.

A crowd clustered on a deck. Waves cracked in. Someone tapped Scott on the arm. "This way," Larry Silverman said, "I want to show you something."

Larry led him to a small room behind a kitchen and snapped on a light to reveal a washing machine, a dryer and a large, canvas clothes hamper. He lifted the floppy lid of the hamper and Scott peered inside.

At first he saw only clothes. His vision adjusted, he made out two people entwined on a pile of sheets and towels.

Scott looked more closely. Deep in the bowels of the clothes hamper, Art Levin and Barbara Feldstein held each other. Unaware, or uncaring that others might see them, they murmured, kissed, snuggled close together.

CHAPTER 25

The Dow Jones Industrial Average edged hopefully toward 1,000, that mystical barrier it had never surmounted, as the November, 1972, Presidential elections approached. On a sunny day in October, Mrs. Lander finally sold her thousand shares of Princeton Group for $1.00 a share.

"That's more than a forty per-cent profit," Scott Lehmann said. She paid 70 cents a share at the beginning of summer and he had thought the stock would never move.

Barry Kalish overheard and poked his head in. Walter Cappeletti passed in the aisle, saw the two of them jovial in Scott's office, and stepped in to join them. "Is it true, six women to every man out there at Davis Park?" Walter knew that Scott had just completed his final weekend at his summer house.

"Six women to one, that's right, and all of them nymphomaniacs," Scott said.

Walter chuckled. "Me, I wasted my single years drinking beer at the Jersey shore, should have gone to Fire Island."

"It's only my first summer out there," Scott said. "Barry here's the veteran."

"I'm didn't go in a house this year," Barry said. "That was a few years back."

Walter turned, interested. "Where on Fire Island?"

"The Pines," Barry said.

"That's a pretty mixed area, isn't it," Walter said.

"What do you mean, 'mixed?'" Barry looked for support to Scott, who – too late – regretted opening his mouth in the first place. "'Mixed.'" Walter wiggled his wrist. "You know."

"That might be," Barry said. "I'm not good at recognizing."

Walter, who judged his brokers on their production and who probably knew Barry's sexual predilection, peered out Scott's window. "Look at that," he said, "I think they've topped off the south tower." He glanced at Scott's painting of the mountain men, mumbled something like, "Go get 'em," and disappeared down the aisle.

"It wasn't six women to every man, it was more like about even," Scott said to Barry. "I didn't score at Davis Park all summer."

"I never went to the Columbia University," Barry said. "I got my degree at City College. My father was not not a furrier. He owned a grocery in the Bronx."

"That's true?"

"As I stand here."

"That's good, you're a man of the people," Scott said.

Monica Corbin looked in. "Scott, a Bill Fosse's on the line. He says he knew you in high school." She swayed on her high heels.

"Yes. I'll talk to him." It seemed to Scott that since their night together Monica communicated to him as a teammate might, as, for example, a shortstop might confer with a third baseman. He had changed too, in that he saw her now more as a fellow professional. He knew that she and Bruce Stanton continued to live together.

Both Scott and Barry observed that Bruce did not wander to this end of the office anymore. Instead he called Monica on the telephone, and Barry maintained that he could tell when it was Bruce by the way she crossed her legs.

Scott picked up the phone. "Bill Fosse. My god." Images from yesteryear tumbled. He recalled a skinny kid, study hall tumult, old cars.

Bill Fosse bought and sold newer vehicles these days, he said. He still lived on Chestnut Street in Grange, Illinois, and occasionally flew to Newark to attend car auctions in New Jersey. "I'm into real estate too, Scott. People say I made a lucky guess on the new Telmark subdivision."

Scott caught the cue. "Lucky guess. Sure."

"Remember Terry McNeely? He bought that tract along the creek next to the country club and put up condos. I said, 'Terry, don't pay the bank twelve per cent, I'll loan you the money at five if you let me take three of those condos on time.'"

"I'll bet this story has a happy ending," Scott said.

"I paid one-ten and sold for one-forty."

"That's what's going out there? I thought you guys swam in the creek and played horseshoes under the elms." It occurred to Scott, sitting there above Wall Street, that this morning he saw a homeless, legless man begging on a subway platform, but it seemed these days that only canny capitalists lived in his old home town. Every time somebody from there called, they had a victory story. Maybe the Bill Fosses of his youth were on to something; maybe this was the start of a new golden age.

"...market looks poised to run," Bill continued. "What stocks do you push these days, ol' buddy?"

"I like computers." Scott paused for effect. He could play this game too. After three years in the brokerage business, he enjoyed cultivating an aura of unseen forces, of knowledge supernatural.

"I'll give you a call when I get back to Grange," Bill Fosse said.

Monica left for lunch. Gary Lincoln, the office's only black broker, wandered down the aisle. "Got a minute, Scott?"

"Sure. Come on in, Gary."

"Scott, you're good with options. A customer of mine wants to write calls against Cashman Drug. Which month would you sell?"

Scott punched up various months and suggested a call four months out. He suspected, though, that his visitor wanted to talk about something else.

"I hear Monica plans to take the brokers' test," Gary said.

"She'll ace it," Scott said.

"What do you think of her moving in with Bruce Stanton?"

"I think Monica can take care of herself."

A memory flashed through Scott's mind, a sales assistant ushered in a white couple to meet Gary. Scott remembered the look of surprise on the couples' faces because they had only spoken on the phone and apparently did not know Gary was black. Gary was not mocha like Monica, Gary was Mississippi black. The white couple left without opening an account. How did Gary do it? How did he handle this stuff?

"...Say Bruce gets tired of her," Gary said.

"Maybe Monica gets tired of him."

"You're not worried?"

"Monica's tough, she knows to cross at the light."

"I hear she does a good job."

"The best sales assistant I've ever had."

Gary rose. "Cashman Drug. I'll mention it to my guy."

Barry Kalish looked in after Gary left. "How do you rate? Gary Lincoln hasn't said more than hello to me in two years."

"He's looking out for Monica," Scott said. "And what have you said to him?"

"'Hi, dark saviour. How about a drink?'"

Scott couldn't help but laugh. "City College, huh?" he said.

"It beats Alcorn Taxidermy or wherever the hell you went."

A customer called, a young attorney. "Scott, I don't think I can listen to another balding society person tell me he doubled his money in the market. Put me into something that will move."

"Intergraphics and National Computer."

"How many shares could I buy?" Scott punched up the credit balance in the account. "You could handle three hundred of each."

"Buy me a hundred of each," the customer said.

Scott wrote the orders and swooshed them away in a pneumatic tube. He leaned back in his chair and gazed out his windows at his view of New York Harbor. He watched the moving numbers on his computer screen. He glanced up at his western painting, so different from the city outside, and pondered for the upteenth time the sun glow on the trees along the river. A setting sun, not rising, he had decided after much contemplation.

These mountain men, he wondered, did they lust for money? Sure they did. But maybe something of honor stirred in them too.

Scott picked up Jennifer at her place. They would share dinner and sex after their weekend apart and she walked with him up Columbus Avenue in her short skirt and shiny shoes.

"We had a ceremony at our house and I burned my bathing suit. Art Levin – you remember him as Lamont Gramercy Cranston – got accepted at NYU Law School."

"I remember him as Art Levin and I admire his ambition in taking on a new career," Jennifer said.

They discussed people they knew, General Brands, the world in general. She likes her job, Scott thought. I'm happy because the stock market climbs. This wine tastes especially good.

They returned to her apartment and she padded about in her underwear. Scott carried her into the bedroom and tied her wrists to the bedposts with scarves. "Don't, don't," she whispered as she thrashed beneath him. She moaned and gripped him with her legs.

He sat afterward on her balcony, looking down at Central Park. Don't take anything for granted, he told himself.

CHAPTER 26

Scott Lehmann's three ZaneCorp clients sat with $400,000 in available money in their accounts. Ever alert to uninvested cash, he telephoned Ingrid Henson and suggested they buy National Computer and Intergraphics.

"I don't know about computers," Ingrid said. "What else do you recommend?"

Scott culled his firm's research reports and called her back. "Argo Aluminum," he said.

He had convinced himself that both the overall market and Argo Aluminum must continue to rise, and such conviction, he knew, made him more persuasive. He knew also that if Ingrid and the others were fully invested, he could equally as well convince himself that stocks must go lower, and with conviction urge them to sell. He knew that this sincerity, and it was sincerity, made him an effective salesman.

"Mr. Crosland wants to buy something," Ingrid said. "Send me what you have on Argo Aluminum."

Scott sped the research report uptown by messenger and within an hour Ingrid responded. "Mr. Crosland doesn't like aluminums. He likes technology. What do you recommend in computer stocks?"

Rather than remind her that this morning he had suggested two computer stocks, National Computer and Intergraphics, Scott determined to build a stronger case. "I'll talk to our technology analyst and get back to you."

Tuttle, Osborn & Durkin advised its brokers not to speak to analysts directly, on the theory that if they did analysts would have no time for anything else. It was tacitly understood, however, that if your name appeared on the Big Producer list, analysts would take your call.

This one did, and Scott asked about his two favorites. "National Computer will soon announce innovative new products," the analyst said. "Intergraphics may provide a nice earnings surprise."

"Is what you're saying generally known on the Street?"

"The Street expects National's new products to open fresh ground. The Street expects Intergraphics to announce a forty-cent second quarter versus eighteen cents last year. I feel the thrust in both companies is stronger than most realize. National's new display terminal will knock your socks off. Intergraphics might do closer to fifty cents than forty. I see two emerging leaders here."

"I've recommended these two stocks to many of my clients," Scott said, "so naturally I wonder if you will mention what you just told me in future research reports."

"I don't tell you anything that I don't tell others," the analyst said. "I want to make that clear. But, yes, I intend in the near future to give both stocks another nudge."

"Thank you very much." Scott jumped up from his desk. Here was good information, and he had unearthed it through his own initiative. George Rogalski would be proud of him. He forgave the analyst, on the spot, for his use of the phrase, "knock your socks off."

He telephoned Ingrid. Damn, only mid-afternoon, but the receptionist said she had left for the day. Well, he had other customers, but first he decided to test his enthusiasm on office cynic Barry Kalish.

Barry burped, as he often did after lunch, and produced from his desk charts depicting the recent price action of both National Computer and Intergraphics. "Identical thigh and scrotum patterns," he said. "No, seriously, look at this: last week each stock broke above its long-term trading range. Call your parents and buy."

An hour remained before the markets closed. Scott spread blue purchase tickets on his desk and worked his telephone. He wrote orders for 100 shares here, 300 shares there. The two stocks up ticked, 1/8, 1/4. He knew Barry next door was buying too.

Scott thought of all that money floating free in the ZaneCorp accounts. What if both stocks shot upward tomorrow? He considered calling Mr. Crosland directly, then changed his mind. Ingrid had warned him, "He doesn't like brokers."

Both stocks closed up on higher than usual volume. Scott Lehmann sat at his desk in lower Manhattan beneath a painting of the mountains of Montana and stared at translucent, moving numbers. He'd had a good day.

Ingrid Henson usually arrived in her office by nine, so next morning, Friday, Scott telephoned at two minutes past.

"She's not coming in today."

"Where is she? Do you know where I can reach her?"

"She didn't leave a number. I'm sorry."

Scott rang Ingrid's home telephone. No answer. Now, unless she contacted him, they might not talk until Monday. The market opened and both National Computer and Intergraphics ticked higher. Scott and Barry each bought stock in their own accounts – perfectly legal – and continued to recommend both companies to their customers.

Brent Hall purchased 50 shares of each. Scott did not call Art Levin, who needed every penny for law school. He took a quick lunch and when he returned both stocks traded another quarter of a point higher. My god, how much more by Monday? He visualized arrows soaring into the sky.

Some of Scott's customers asked him to make their buy and sell decisions for them. Wall Street defined buying or selling for a customer without his or her specific approval as "exercising discretion." Tuttle, Osborn & Durkin theoretically prohibited this, but many of the firm's veteran brokers often exercised discretion. Management knew this and tacitly looked the other way.

Scott had worked closely with Ingrid for two years and they knew each other well. He imagined her disappointment Monday if he did nothing and both stocks continued to climb.

The timid do not win private offices. The timid do not rank as Big Producers. Ingrid had told him that Mr. Crosland wanted to purchase computer shares for the three ZaneCorp accounts and so Scott decided to do it for them.

He wrote blue buy tickets for 2,000 shares of National Computer and Intergraphics for Mr. Crosland, 1,000 of each for Mr. Irvin, and 300 of each for Ingrid. Even with these purchases, ample cash still remained in each account. Scott pictured Ingrid's pleasure on Monday.

But the moment he entered the orders he began to worry. He bought the stocks at three o'clock and in the last hour of trading the market began to decline. National Computer and Intergraphics dropped an eighth here, a quarter there, giving up their earlier gains. Each tumbled more than a point by the close. Scott had purchased near the highs for the day, and Ingrid did not call.

He must inform her, somehow, that he had without authorization invested several hundred thousand dollars for the ZaneCorp accounts. He must tell her that Mr. Crosland sat on a paper loss of over $4,000, Mr. Irvin $2,000 and she herself about $700.

He was confident National Computer and Intergraphics would continue to rise. They would open strong on Monday and everything would be fine. He would tell Ingrid that his firm's analyst liked both stocks and intended to issue new buy recommendations soon. He acted aggressively, Scott told himself, but with his customers' best interests in mind.

He walked down the hill toward the Rector Street subway station. Fluffball clouds drifted in a blue October sky and the towers of the new World Trade Center glittered in the sun.

Why did he rush to buy those two stocks? Why didn't he just look outside and regard this autumn sky, this slow, regal roll of the seasons?

He had done a stupid thing, and Monday seemed years, eons away.

—

CHAPTER 27

Scott Lehmann scanned the news Monday morning for clues as to how the markets would open and saw nothing to suggest a definite trend in either direction. Barry Kalish stuck his head in to say good morning.

"What do you think, Barry, do National Computer and Intergraphics rally early or rally late?"

"Either, or; every day's a buying opportunity with those two." Barry cocked his head at the painting over Scott's desk. "You wonder how those guys shaved," he said.

"A sharpened grizzly claw, an arrowhead." Scott wanted to relax, and he looked afresh at Charlie Russell's three mountain men. But rather than the solace, the grandeur, he usually took from the painting, today he saw danger. Armed Indians approached. The golden leaves of the trees along the river suggested snow and oncoming winter.

He had tried unsuccessfully to reach Ingrid Henson at home over the weekend. He and Jennifer Cohen jogged in Central Park Saturday and explored roads along the Hudson River above West Point Sunday, but something held him back, he did not mention his problem with the ZaneCorp customers. He told himself they could draw moral lessons and tisk-tisk about it later when all was righted.

He called ZaneCorp at nine o'clock and asked for Ingrid.

"She's traveling. We expect her back this afternoon."

"Please, this is extremely important. I need to reach her."

"I'll ask her to contact you if we hear from her."

Scott stared out his window. Ingrid's unavailability raised a new hope in his mind; a morning market rally might solve his problem before he even told her there was a problem.

But stocks opened lower, and National Computer and Intergraphics continued to drop in price as the day wore on. "A chance to get in on a dip," Barry Kalish repeated on the telephone. Scott heard him continue to recommend both stocks to his customers.

Scott had not told Barry or anyone else that he purchased National Computer and Intergraphics in the ZaneCorp accounts without the customers' consent, and thus he suffered alone. Each downtick stung like a cut in his arm. He realized, as the day wore on and Ingrid did not call, that the longer he waited the more the situation might worsen, and that he absolutely must tell Walter Cappaletti.

Meanwhile he stalled for time and hoped for a rally. He telephoned the securities analyst with whom he talked on Thursday. "When will you reiterate your buy recommendations on National Computer and Intergraphics?"

"Maybe later this week, maybe next week. Don't pin me down. Look, if you own the stocks show some patience. I'm not recommending them as two-day plays."

Scott rode the elevator down to street level, bought a cup of tea and an apple raisin muffin and walked back upstairs. Rule number one in the brokerage business read, "Know your customer," with all the ramifications that implied. For two years he and Ingrid had exchanged ideas, for two years she and the other ZaneCorp people had profited handsomely. Surely now they could stand a day or two of pain.

He glimpsed through his open door a high heel dangling. His telephone rang. "Scott, the Bank," Monica called.

It was 2:46 p.m. and over an hour of trading remained for the day. "Ingrid, where were you? I've been trying to reach you."

"So I heard. What's so important?"

Scott glanced outside before he answered. The October sun glinted on New York Harbor. It was a beautiful day. "I called our computer analyst after you and I talked Thursday; remember, you told me Mr. Crosland wanted to buy computer stocks..." He paused to give Ingrid a chance to anticipate, to help him along, but she said nothing.

"The analyst told me he plans to publicly increase his earnings estimates on National Computer and Intergaphics," Scott continued. "He told me National's got a hot new display terminal, something not generally known on The Street. This analyst has a following, and his recommendations move stocks. I tried to reach you Friday but they said you had left for the weekend, so I went ahead and bought shares in each company for you, Mr. Crosland and Mr. Irvin."

Scott waited. "How many shares?" Ingrid asked.

He told her. "What did you pay and where are they now?"

He told her. Together they did the arithmetic: at current prices the cumulative loss in the three accounts topped $14,000. "I'm sorry, Scott. I can't accept these trades."

"I spoke with the analyst again an hour ago, Ingrid. I'm recommending National Computer and Intergraphics to my other clients and I bought some for myself. I think soon a lot of people will want to own these stocks."

"You should have talked to me first, Scott."

"I know I should have talked to you, but I did what I thought you would have wanted me to do. I did what I thought you would have told me to do had you been here to answer my calls. It's a loss today, sure, but we may rally tomorrow. We may rally for a month."

"Scott, you did these trades without my permission."

"What if the stocks were up now, instead of down?"

"They're not. But that's not the point; I won't accept these trades."

"You want me to bust them? That means I get management involved."

"Do what you have to do. Get management involved. I do not accept these trades."

Scott stepped from his office and Monica sensed something.

"Yes?" she asked.

"Difficulties." He rapped on office manager Walter Cappaletti's door and Walter beckoned him in, listened, frowned, and scratched numbers on a pad. "You should have told me earlier."

Scott listened as Walter grabbed a telephone and instructed a Tuttle, Osborn & Durkin representative on the floor of the New York Stock Exchange. "That's right. Sell at the market. Right now." He turned to Scott. "What's her name, Ingrid? You don't talk to her anymore. From now on our lawyers do the talking."

"Walter, she's my link with my two biggest customers."

The older man sighed. "You did these trades Friday? Why the hell didn't you tell me then?"

"I didn't think I had a problem."

"Scott, I want you to write me a statement describing in detail exactly what happened and when it happened. I want you to have it on my desk tomorrow morning."

Scott returned to his desk. He told himself that he and Ingrid talked almost daily on the telephone for the last two years, that he took her to lunches, sent her flowers on her birthdays. They could clear this up somehow.

In a few minutes Walter summoned him back. "I talked to your 'friend.' Some friend. They want their money back."

"What do we do?" Scott asked.

"It's not 'we,' it's me, and I have no choice, I have to give it to them. Fourteen thousand and change."

"Who pays?"

"You know better than to ask that," Walter said. "Now, here's what's going to happen. Tomorrow you will meet with Cyril Beaton and Aaron Springer and one of our lawyers."

"Why a lawyer?"

"We must, when we do a cash settlement with a customer, report it to the New York Stock Exchange and to the Securities

Exchange Commission. We think it wiser to make a show of rep-rimanding you than to leave it to them."

Scott exhaled.

"Watch out for Springer," Walter said, "he's building a repu-tation as Mr. Clean." He leaned back and toyed with a pencil. He looked at Scott and for the first time appeared to soften. "How much money do you have?"

"Twenty thousand and change in my trading account." Scott deposited his pay checks directly into his brokerage account at Tuttle, Osborn & Durkin. He had invested about ten thousand in tax free bonds and roughly an equal amount in stocks.

"That makes it easier," Walter said, "we know you're good for it. I'll ask you in a day or two to write us a check. That's a lot less embarrassing than deducting from your monthly pay."

Scott gazed out the window at New York Harbor. He had worked hard to prove himself among the Ivy Leaguers, but now, suddenly, he felt the hayseed again. "Any other advice for tomor-row's meeting?" he asked.

"Just tell them what happened. Don't embellish. Don't bull shit. I'll do what I can to protect you. Remember, I need your statement first thing in the morning."

"Thanks, Walter." Scott rose to go.

"You like your new office?" the older man asked.

"I do."

"Don't screw up again if you want to keep it."

CHAPTER 28

Cyril Beaton sat in the biggest chair, frosting in his hair, tassels on his loafers. "Come in, Scott, come in." Beaton served as sales vice president for Tuttle, Osborn and Durkin and pictures of him and his pals playing golf and hoisting trophy fish adorned the walls. Scott thought of this building as waterfront glitz, but he had walked only two blocks from his own office to get here.

A dark, tightly-buttoned man paced the room. "Scott Lehmann, Aaron Springer." Beaton introduced Scott to the firm's new regional sales chairman, who nodded and did not offer to shake hands.

"This is Jeffrey, an attorney in our compliance department." A tall young man rose, extended his hand, and settled in a chair in a corner.

Springer inhaled, rose on his toes. "Gentlemen, our purpose is not to decide whether to reimburse Mr. Lehmann's customers, for that of course we will do. Today, rather, we must consider disciplinary action."

Cyril Beaton unfolded his fingers. "Well, Aaron, since you've already begun..." he said, ironical, it seemed to Scott, and he took heart at his tone. This is Aaron's show, Beaton's manner suggested, but he reminded them all that he, Beaton, ranked higher in the chain of command.

Springer bounded, literally bounded, on the balls of his feet. "Lehmann, you initiated these trades without consulting your customers?"

"I've worked with these clients for over two years. They wanted to buy computer stocks. I talked to our analyst and he recommended Intergraphics and National Computer. I could not reach the clients, so I took it upon myself to buy the stocks for them." Scott sought to make what he had done sound the most natural thing in the world.

"Took it upon yourself!" Springer swept them all with a glittering glance. "How long have you been with us, Lehmann?"

"Three years."

"Three years, and you invested over two hundred thousand dollars without bothering to speak to the customers?"

"I was wrong. I realize that. I won't make that mistake again." Scott looked them one-by-one in the eye. He sought to both tell the truth and to sound contrite, for he understood that when the regional chairman intoned, "Protect the public," everybody straight to the top of the firm had no choice but to snap to attention.

"Aaron," Cyril Beaton broke in, "I think we should consider the entirety of his record. I believe, Scott, that in your three years with us you received only one previous complaint and that was disposed of as specious?"

"Yes, sir, that's correct," Scott said.

"What was that other complaint," Springer asked.

"I was accused of overtrading," Scott said.

"You were accused of churning?" Springer used the common term.

"Wait, Aaron," Beaton said. "Tell us, Scott, why that complaint was dismissed."

"I showed that the trades followed our firm's own recommendations."

At this, Scott saw the young attorney, who until now had jotted desultory notes, glance up and rouse himself.

"Lehmann," Springer said, "I worked as a retail broker for fourteen years. Not once in those fourteen years did a client ever accuse me of churning."

Scott saw Cyril Beaton glance at his watch. "Jeffrey," Beaton asked the young attorney, "do you want to comment here?"

Jeffrey removed his glasses and held them in his right hand. "Mr. Lehmann, of course, must make the losses good from his own pocket," he said. "The amount involved is over fourteen thousand dollars and that in itself constitutes some punishment."

"Bull shit, Jeffrey..." Springer began.

The attorney lifted his hand, as if for attention, and continued, "In the event of further disciplinary action by our firm, Mr. Lehmann would have the right to request a hearing from the New York Stock Exchange. That would involve some time and effort on all our parts." He glanced around at each of them.

Beaton looked at Springer. "Aaron?"

"I think there are times when it is beneficial to set an example."

"Well, this young man's mistake cost him fourteen thousand dollars," Beaton said. "That's an example."

Springer turned to Scott. "Out of curiosity," he said, "where do those two stocks trade today?"

"Higher," Scott said, "both up over a point, I believe."

Springer gazed out a window. "Okay, Cy," he said, "let it stand."

The young attorney, who seemed to Scott about his own age, a person he might encounter at a Sixish on Fire Island, accompanied him outside. "What did Springer want?" Scott asked him.

The attorney hesitated before replying. "He wanted to suspend you for six months."

"Thanks for not endorsing that idea."

"I only offered an opinion." The attorney turned and walked away down the hall. Maybe, like Art Levin, he once wanted to do good for the meek and humble, Scott mused, but now he spends his days protecting overpaid evildoers like me.

He strolled in gentle sunshine back to his office. A breeze blew from New York Harbor. Wall Street seemed deserted, but

Scott knew that in buildings all around him people bought and sold, not interested at all in the weather.

He glanced at the sky and realized another month had passed. Days blended one with another, summer gave way to autumn. It was still warm enough, he ought to take a week off and go to the beach. He'd ask Jennifer, there'd be hardly anybody there. They'd share long sunsets, loll at restaurants, listen to the wash of waves.

Or he could bring his camping gear and he and Jennifer would drive north to the Adirondacks. They would sleep together in that same motel where they stayed in July and climb Giant or Algonquin or some of the other big mountains. The bugs would be gone, the nights would be cool. It would be special up there this time of year.

He rode an elevator up to his office. "How did it go?" Barry Kalish asked.

"I make good the losses. I remain in the fray."

Monica Corbin stepped briskly in. "Mr. Polinsky wants you to call. Here's your other messages. Everything okay?"

"I think so, thanks," Scott said. He saw that the market continued its rally while he was away. Intergraphics and National Computer had climbed back to where they were when he purchased them in the ZaneCorp accounts on Friday.

I'll learn from this, Scott thought. I'll work hard and replace the accounts I lost. "Monica," he called, "I'll need two thousand of those muni prospecting letters."

"That's a lot of envelopes."

"I'll take a box home with me tonight." Monica sometimes addressed prospecting envelopes for him, but tonight he wanted to do it himself. He saw himself selecting names of residents between East Forty-Second and East Ninety-Sixth Streets from the Manhattan telephone book. He'd make a game of it, a lottery. He pictured several hours of redeeming effort.

Walter Cappaletti rapped and entered and tilted his head to study Scott's Charlie Russell painting. "Where's that supposed to be?" He had asked this before.

"Montana."

"I like more trees myself. Scott, I talked to Cy Beaton and he told me Springer relented. I'm not surprised, I wasn't worried."

"You weren't? I was."

Walter lowered his voice. "You're a Big Producer," he said. "Nobody wants to lose a Big Producer."

CHAPTER 29

Scott Lehmann sat at lunchtime with Art Levin on the steps of the Federal Building. "Assume, Lamont, that a stockbroker fears for his soul, that he wants in atonement to serve humanity. Assume he decides, as you have, to pursue the study of law."

"Fear not, Storm, the legal profession is not so sacred it would be tainted by the likes of you."

"Walk me through it," Scott said, for the thought of becoming a legal lion had occurred to him in the night. He visualized grateful widows, not unattractive, and a high-rise penthouse. He imagined sleek Jennifer home from a General Brands board meeting and cute, round-eyed moppets.

"First you take the Law School Aptitude Test," Art said. "You ask law schools to send you applications. I began with Columbia University, Brooklyn Law, St. John's and N.Y.U."

"Age? Does it matter?"

"I'm twenty-nine and I start classes in January. People go to law school when they are fifty."

"What happens when you begin?"

"First year, like everybody else, I take torts, real property, contracts, basic criminal law. Second year I seek my individual path. There's securities law, there's international or corporate law, there's trusts and estates. I'm thinking environmental and public law. Legal research, musty tomes; let's find those paupers decent homes. You consider a career change, Lash Storm?"

"Sounding possibilities, Lamont, sounding possibilities." Scott wanted to think there was no profession he could not master, no summit he could not climb. But he suspected, as Art spoke, that here he indulged in another whimsy, as once he had rushed to audition for television commercials. He returned to his office with a cup of tea and an apple raisin muffin.

"Who's Mrs. Lander?" Barry Kalish asked. "For twenty minutes I look up penny stocks."

"We're professionals," Scott said. "We help the little people."

It was a cool day, ideal autumn weather, and he and Jennifer Cohen played tennis late that afternoon amid the wreckage of the Lower East Side. Everything looked bolted, scarred. The East River rushed by.

Puerto Ricans and blacks competed at softball on an adjoining field. They slapped hands and purpled the air with epithets while on nearby tennis courts Caucasians in white clothes swatted fluffy yellow balls to and fro. The contrast stuck Scott. He and Jennifer departed before dark.

She changed at his apartment and he took her to dinner at a tiny restaurant on West Tenth Street. "I've been wanting to try this place," he said. "Expect a tiny waitress, tiny plates."

She scanned the menu. "Not tiny prices though."

A normal-size waitress appeared and Scott, Jennifer and several other couples dined in intimacy. Outside a north wind flailed at the windows; inside candle flames flickered and the world seemed an orderly place.

"The computer stocks I bought for your dad inch ahead. Did he tell you he opened an account?"

"He mentioned it," Jennifer said, "no details. We don't really communicate that often."

"I don't talk that much with my parents either," Scott said. He intended to tell Jennifer about his ZaneCorp fiasco - to roll it about, try to clarify in his mind exactly what happened and why

– and now seemed an opportune moment. But he could not bring himself to broach the subject.

"Call your parents," she said. "It's easy."

Scott shook his head. "Two of them. If I call one, then I feel I should call the other."

"They're divorced, you said?"

"Fifteen years. Mother lives in the same old house and dad rents a new place a few blocks away on the same street. He sells farm equipment."

"Was there another man, another woman?"

"I don't think so," Scott said. "They just wore each other out."

"People adjust," Jennifer said. "My mother said it would kill her when she and dad divorced and now she goes on singles' cruises and does water aerobics."

They strolled out into the early darkness of late October and meandered up Eighth Avenue. A north wind hinted at firs and frosts and Scott sniffed the air excitedly. "Smell that? There's a whiff of Canada." He frowned at the traffic on Fourteenth Street. "Once it was all forest," he said.

"'Once it was all forest.' That's my Scott."

She slept over at his place, choosing a nightie from her designated Jennifer drawer. She let an arm drop on the sheets, kerplunk, and he smiled because she did that all the time.

"What's so funny, tousled toodle?"

He dropped an arm, kerplunk.

"Do I do that?"

"Who's the tousled toodle? You're the tousled toodle," he said.

Scott made reservations at a motel in Montauk and they drove Saturday morning to the eastern tip of Long Island where land stopped and cliffs rose from the sea. It was warmer than yesterday and the sun shone. He flung open their terrace door and waves pounded virtually beneath their feet.

"The ocean's too noisy," Scott said. "We'll call the office and see about getting some sound barriers set up."

"No, I like listening..." Jennifer began, and then realized he jested.

They carried a blanket to a beach where a few weeks ago throngs frolicked and today only a few wizened stalwarts remained. The water looked gray in the pale, slanting sun. Scott splashed out a step or two, retreated and lay on the blanket. "I'm absorbing warmth for winter," he said.

Jennifer touched his arm. "Cavalier wants our Le Gourmet line."

"How big is Cavalier?"

"Two hundred and twenty stores. It's my first big sale." She recited profit projections while incoming tide erased footprints in the sand.

They waded into the water again. Horizons and fishing boats appeared more sharply edged, more finite than during the summer. A chilly breeze quickened and, shivering, they hurried to their room for a hot shower. Scott lathered her square, little shoulders and pointy breasts.

He lay on the bed, absorbed in watching a ship slide out of sight over the curve of earth and ocean, while Jennifer next to him wielded a droning, electric hair dryer. Her dreamy look of involvement as she smoothed and pampered herself reminded him of the day they hiked along the Opalescent River.

Scott closed his eyes. He felt a blast of hot electric dryer air agitate his flaccid, resting member.

They drove for dinner to a restaurant in the old whaling port of Sag Harbor but even on this off-season Saturday had to wait at the bar for a table. They sat at barstools and watched a red sun descend into Great Peconic Bay. "He's not sophisticated in cameras and cars," a young woman at a table behind them said.

An older couple sat along the bar next to Jennifer. The man wore a leisure suit and the woman pink pants. "Talk about scared, the doctor told me I had cancer," the woman said to the bartender. "I ran out and spent four thousand dollars on a fur coat. Ralph let me do it, bless his soul; he knew I always wanted a fur coat."

"Cancer? You look pretty healthy to me," the bartender said.

"The doctor took new tests and told me he made a mistake. I didn't have cancer after all."

Ralph hugged her. "She kept the coat, though," he said.

Scott looked at Jennifer and she looked back at him. "That was a nice story," she said.

They got a table and ordered lobster and clinked glasses. A full moon illuminated the parking lot when they walked outside. "Perfect night. Let's drive around and look at houses," Jennifer suggested.

They passed old trees and sea-captain homes pocked by forgotten storms. Scott turned a corner and saw an unlighted playground with a basketball court. He parked, leaped out and rummaged in his car trunk for his old basketball.

Jennifer removed her bracelets and flung two-handed set shots. They played basketball by the light of the moon. Scott feinted as if to dribble around her. "Oh no you don't." She blocked his way in her flat, shiny shoes.

Two kids pedaled past on bicycles, turned, came back. Scott heard their low voices as they sat on their bikes and watched.

He drove a back road toward their motel and switched off the headlights for a moment. His car hurtled through vague, black obstacles, tree shadows across the road.

Waves pounded in below their terrace, and they slid open the glass door and sat outside facing the ocean. "I did an unintelligent thing at work," Scott said.

"Yes?"

He described his ill-timed purchases in the ZaneCorp accounts, emphasizing how he tried repeatedly to reach Ingrid before acting.

"Then what happened?"

"I met with management." Scott spoke slowly in the darkness. "I got hit for the damages. I lost the accounts and one of our execs wanted to suspend me for six months but he got overruled."

"You got off lucky," Jennifer said.

"You think so?"

"Sure. You traded without authorization." She knew the brokerage business.

He felt foolish. Could this conversation be about him, Scott Lehmann, Big Producer? "What do you think those ZaneCorp people would have done if the stocks went up instead of down? They would have kept them, of course. In fact, both stocks are higher now than when we bought them."

"That's not the point," Jennifer said. "You're supposed to know situations."

It seemed to Scott, in the darkness of the terrace, that she glanced at him harshly. "You never made a mistake at work?" he shot back.

"Sure, I've made mistakes; no need to get defensive."

"You're acting so damn officious about it."

They quarreled. Scott lost his temper. Jennifer turned her face away. "I felt so safe with you at first," she said.

"You don't now?"

"I feel...I don't know. It's like when you turned out the car lights and drove down the highway in the dark."

They talked, they calmed, they turned toward bed. Scott held her arms above her head while she squirmed and fought him. They tussled again in the morning to the sound of the sea.

They lingered over breakfast and strolled on the beach. Gray clouds raced and a cold wind blew. They drove back to the city listening to a New York Giants football game on the radio.

They wanted to move, to exercise after sitting in the the car, so they changed at her place and loped across the street into Central Park. They ran twice around the reservoir, left the park at Seventy-Second Street and trotted down Central Park West. Scott thought how this street, these trees, linked now with Jennifer in his mind.

She had not spoken for a while and he glanced at her. "Any thoughts on next weekend?"

"Not yet. You?"

"I'd like to go hiking," Scott said.

"Call me," Jennifer said.

CHAPTER 30

The wind blew and it rained outside. Scott telephoned Brent Hall at his new office at *Business World,* waited for a secretary to put him through, and suggested they play basketball at the Leroy Street gym.

"I've got my gym stuff right here," Brent said. "It's been sitting next to my waste basket for the last two weeks."

Scott subwayed north to the familiar, fetid locker room and shot baskets until Brent's face appeared at the top of the circular stairs. "Who's this?" His friend looked chubbier and aw-shucks contrite.

"Staff meetings, trivia – I really haven't been exercising like I should."

"Well no wonder, by god," Scott said. "*Business World* flung the whole Northeast at you. Maine. Pennsylvania. New York City alone would be enough for most men."

"If the truth be told," Brent said. "New York City *is* the Northeast Region."

Other regulars arrived, shooed neighborhood kids off the main court and started a game. Brent had not played in several weeks and he missed his first few shots, but soon his touch returned. He chased up and down the gym's polished floor with his old fanaticism.

They won some, they lost some, and showered afterward in a roar of splash and steam. "I've got to do this more often," Brent said.

"How's Ruth?"

"Busy. She sends her greeting."

"I take it you recommend marriage." Scott offered his friend a covert chance to complain.

"It's pleasant once you get used to having another person around."

They pulled on their street clothes and combed their hair. Brent wanted to talk stocks. He edited an article on a new gasoline pump: "You set it to fill your tank automatically while you wash your windshield or stare at the sky. I wrote down the names of the two companies that stand to profit the most; could you check them out for me, Scott? Ruth and I might want to invest."

"I will, I'll call you; I'm looking for ideas myself."

They climbed concrete stairs to the street outside. Trucks and cars edged in a miasma of exhaust fumes down Seventh Avenue toward the Holland Tunnel.

"Steamers and sangria," Scott suggested.

Brent looked at his watch. "Next time." No subway today: he hailed a cab for the trip to his new conjugal apartment on the East Side.

A vagrant asked Scott for money. He gave the man a dollar. He saw an old woman sleeping on a bench beneath a newspaper she pulled over her body for warmth. "STOCK MARKET PUSHES TOWARD NEW HIGHS," proclaimed the headline.

Scott researched the stocks Brent mentioned and telephoned him the next day. "Titan looks the stronger of the two. In fact, I may suggest it to some of my customers." He considered buying shares for himself, but after making good the ZaneCorp losses little loose money remained in his brokerage account.

Brent bought a hundred Titan shares jointly for himself and Ruth. They shared a joint account now, common with married couples, and she had transferred in assets of her own. If either died, the other automatically inherited whatever the account contained.

The new World Trade Center dominated his view and Scott glanced at it for the twentieth time today. Winter approached and workmen scurried to enclose the upper floors of the south tower.

He missed the old days of meeting Art Levin for lunch on the steps of the Federal Building; these days his friend attended classes on torts and common law. Scott telephoned him that night.

"I become a drudge, Storm, a haunter of legal libraries; my social life atrophies for want of use."

"The wind carries tales, Lamont, of clothes hampers imprinted with the forms of you and Barbara Feldstein."

"Flagon of beer, spirit of gin; yes I'll admit I've seen her again."

Scott pressed for details, but Art confessed only to attending a few brotherly-sisterly movies. "What about you and Jennifer? Did you call dad and hold him to his monied promise?"

"I did, as you aptly advised. He opened an account."

"You see? Next he'll suggest golf at Burning Tree. Take lessons in putting, Storm."

Scott telephoned Jennifer Cohen. His birthday approached, and, she suggested they postpone their proposed hike in the northern woods. Instead, she pledged to buy him dinner Friday if he opened three new accounts this week. "I've already opened four," he said.

"Well good. I would have treated you anyway; that's the kind of warm person I am. I picked a place. You'll see."

He wore a sports jacket and tie and rode a subway north to Columbus Circle. Jennifer awaited him at her door in a black knit dress, black stockings and high heels.

"Fine, Jennifer, fine," he said.

She handed their cab driver a written address and they sped down Broadway through Times Square. The mood of the city changed below Forty-Second, as if they had entered another cultural zone, and the same thing happened below Fourteenth. Scott guessed she chose a bistro in Greenwich Village, but they continued on down Broadway. "Where? What?"

"You'll see."

They crossed Manhattan Bridge, turned north along the water and stopped at a restaurant on the Brooklyn bank of the East River. She had reserved a table with a panoramic view of the Manhattan skyline.

Scott hoisted a glass of red wine and admired the towers of Gotham silhouetted against a purple sky. "This city," he said; "it's more home to me now than my little town in Illinois."

Jennifer smiled amid her clingy wool. "You go first," she suggested. They liked to launch their Friday nights by bringing each other up to date.

"Monica begins broker training soon, meaning Barry and I must break in a new sales assistant unless we can pilfer someone experienced from the rookies. Brent Hall and I played basketball and already his new job at *Business Week* spins off investment ideas." He described Brent's fuel pump discovery.

"Ruth?"

"Brent says she likes it up on East Eighty-Sixth Street. I talked to Art Levin. Rember Barbara Feldstein? They're dating now."

Jennifer grinned. "Virgin volume, something running; no surprise, I saw that coming." She had Art's intonation down perfectly.

Scott laughed. "All of us claim now that we suspected." He asked Jennifer about her week, expecting blow-by-blows of intraoffice skirmishes.

"I'm the official pigeon feeder," she surprised him. Office cohorts discovered a nest of these birds near a corner window at General Brands. Jennifer volunteered as nourishment consultant. She experimented – popcorn, bird seed, bread crumbs – and issued daily progress reports.

Scott sat back bemused. Sometimes, since his ZaneCorp fiasco, it seemed to him that Jennifer eyed him warily. Not tonight. Tonight her warm glances suggested she trusted him implicitly.

Well, it was his birthday. He might test her tolerance and discuss ages – his 28, her's nearing 26. Once before, when he mentioned babies and ages in the same sentence, she accused him of clubbing her with the dread biological clock.

Jennifer jumped up just as he prepared his serious look. "Excuse me. I've a phone call to make."

Scott watched a tugboat pass and listened to people at the next table discuss the stock market. Would the Dow Jones Industrials finally close above 1,000? He wanted to lean across and say something riveting. He wanted to predict the exact day, the exact hour.

Jennifer returned, smoothed her napkin. "Apartment vacant in my building. I promised to notify someone..."

"Pigeon feeder. Now housing consultant. Where's that old, slashing corporate climber?"

"Well, you know, sometimes by being nice..."

They taxied after dinner to the Clarion in Soho, Barry Kalish's latest disco discovery. Determined to perform in her high heels, Jennifer tilted forward and stutter-stepped to the music. Scott's groin tingled as he watched. She concentrated, her lips half open. The tip of her tongue darted moistly out.

They left around midnight and necked like teenagers on the couch at her apartment. She stripped to her bra and panties and he carried her into the bedroom. "Happy birthday, Scott." She spread her arms. He reached for something to tie her hands.

They jogged Sunday amid the autumn reds and golds of Central Park. Jennifer cooked lasagna and they sipped an Italian red on her terrace. "October's my favorite month," Scott said. They made plans to hike the Catskills next weekend.

She telephoned him Wednesday at his office. "My old Cornell roomie called. She drives up from Baltimore Friday afternoon and I told her she could stay at my place. I'm to seek tickets for available Broadway shows and kind of lead her around over the weekend. I hope you don't mind."

"We can hike another time," Scott said. He glanced at his painting of the mountain men. "I'm thinking about renting a ski house. This would be a good time for me to drive up to Vermont and look around." The idea had just seized him.

"I could talk to my friend. She might want to meet you."

"Another time," he said. "Enjoy."

❖ ❖ ❖

CHAPTER 31

Jennifer Cohen and her college roomie dined out on the town Friday night. Brent Hall and Ruth hosted Scott Lehmann and several of Ruth's fellow speech therapists for dinner.

Scott left before nine, arose early Saturday morning and drove five hours to Killington Mountain in Vermont. He followed a winding access road past restaurants and chalets and the old house, converted now to a real estate office, that served for years as the home of the family that farmed this high, cold valley. He parked at the foot of the sprawling Killington Ski Area.

It was a warm for late October and the sun felt good on his face. Scott stood on a deck outside the base lodge in hiking shorts and sweat shirt and stared up at the mountain. "Do it," he thought. He set out to climb a trail called Superstar that he last skied in March, seven months before.

He toiled upward through brown grass, surprised at the steepness, to the crest of a knoll that rose sharply above the base lodge. He stopped, breathing hard, and gazed still higher at the skyline of the Green Mountains.

Scott learned to ski in Illinois on a hill that descended maybe 300 feet from the terminal moraine outside town. He never in those days, skiing in the Midwest, plunged down anything remotely this steep. Then he moved to New York and discovered New England. Killington, one of many areas up here, dropped over 3,000 feet from top to bottom.

Scott climbed again. The sensation of sun on the backs of his calf muscles reminded him of high school and college football practices. He remembered the smell of stained shoulder pads and the sting of sweat on his face. He remembered watching footballs rise against autumn skies and waiting for those footballs to come down.

"What is skiing like?" Barry Kalish asked him one day last winter.

"It's like running with a football and suddenly you break out into the open field," Scott, the former fullback, replied.

Barry looked puzzled. Probably he never busted free running with a football in the open field. But that's the way skiing was. It was powder snow kicking white dust behind you on a crisp, blue-sky day.

It was cold on your face and beer in the bar later and early morning halos that ringed the sun.

Scott climbed higher. Superstar's twists and turns reminded him of another of his favorite Vermont trails, Spruce at Stratton. Both offered steeps and sudden surprise. Both offered *character*. Killington would eventually change Superstar's name to Ovation, and reassign the name Superstar to a still steep but straighter and wider trail. But on this October day Scott Lehmann did not know that.

He looked down and imagined himself alone on a great, white mountain. It was winter, he had suffered a serious injury, and the gods granted him one last run. "Which will it be?" the head god asked.

"Superstar," Scott answered.

"You may begin," the head god said.

Scott imagined he pushed hard with his ski poles and launched himself from the brink. He swooshed the steepness and swerved to a stop at the top of the final plunge, the spot where he now stood. He looked down at the base lodge. He examined the sky. He leaned forward on his poles. He felt strength in his arms, his legs. He kicked off down that final waterfall.

His spine tingled, imagining this last great boon the gods had granted. He hiked higher, on up to a wooded ridge near the summit of Killington Mountain where Superstar began.

Life goes too fast, he thought. The geese fly south, you get the basketball on the fast break and lay it soft against the glass. You buckle your skis in blue, morning cold. You laugh in the night and one day your body tells you you are old.

Scott walked back down the way he had come, fading leaves of autumn clicking past in the wind. Skiing would not begin up here for another month, and only a few cars dotted the parking lot today. Reluctant to leave, he hiked another, shorter trail. He walked to his car and gazed up at the mountain.

Scott liked at the end of a ski day to lift his ski poles and tap them together in a salute to the mountain. He had not skied today, but he decided to observe tradition just the same. He looked up at the summit of Killington Mountain. He lifted his wrists, struck them several times together. The mountain seemed to smile.

He drove to a real estate office, got a listing of ski house rentals, and followed back roads to look at several. The houses looked drab with no snow around them, unpainted, their parking lots dusty. He peered in windows and poked around. Now if Jennifer asked him: yes, he looked. He did not find anything he wanted to rent.

If you rented a ski house, you felt you had to use it. If you stayed in motels, you could ski Vermont one weekend, New Hampshire, Maine or somewhere else the next. Scott took a motel room for the night, ate alone at a restaurant on the access road and wondered what Jennifer did in the city.

It was Saturday night, so he drove to a bar with a lot of cars outside. Young couples gyrated to a loud, local band and a swinging door led to a separate area that included billiard tables and restrooms. He struck up a conversation with a young woman in tight jeans. "What do you do?" she asked.

"I'm a stockbroker."

"Do you have a house in the area?"

"I'm looking. What about you?"

"I'm waiting for my boyfriend." They danced. Outside cold peaks pierced the sky.

The boyfriend arrived. Scott danced with other women. From habit, he wrote a phone number on the back of a napkin. But he felt out of practice, not sufficiently motivated, and finally he walked outside alone.

Wind stirred through miles of pines and he gazed up at the dark shape of Killington Mountain. It struck him that for three years he had not taken a vacation that lasted longer than a week.

Why not? It was not that he feared to miss a special stock offering or four or five days' commissions. It was not that there was no place he wanted to go. It was the action, he realized. He had not wanted to miss the action. For three years he had worried that if he took more than a week off he might lose the trader's feel, the invisible thread. For three years he had lived and breathed to the tom-tom of money.

Scott tried to stand perfectly still and to listen to his heartbeat. He looked up at the sky and tried to remember the voice that called to him in the Adirondacks.

Did it still want to reach him? To warn him? To tell him something?

Maybe if he waited, if he gave it a chance. Scott stood in the darkness and listened. No, the voice did not call to him now.

CHAPTER 32

"How did your reunion go with college roomie?"

"The usual touristy things. Did you drive up to Vermont?"

"I did. I climbed my favorite ski trail at Killington."

"Did you look at ski houses?"

"Several," Scott said, "but they look kind of desolate without snow." He spoke from his office, where Jennifer Cohen telephoned him Monday morning.

He had thought things over and he wanted to do something with Jennifer next weekend, go somewhere, reclaim her, isolate her one on one. "Did you ever go to a football game while you were a student at Cornell?" he asked. She had graduated from there four years ago.

"No," Jennifer said. "Is that what they did at that big, noisy round place?"

"The stadium. Yes. I have never visited Cornell and I want to. Dartmouth plays football there next Saturday. We could watch the game and hike in the Catskills Sunday. What do you say?"

"I'm excited," Jennifer said.

"Excellent."

"I bring my hiker clothes?"

"Yes. Something warm. There's no pity up on Black Dome. I'll come for you Friday about six. We can stay somewhere on the way up."

Barry Kalish passed by Scott's office whistling. The stock market continued to rally as the Presidential election approached. Republicans – and most Wall Streeters called themselves Republicans – rubbed their hands in anticipation of friends in high places. Richard Nixon pledged to end the war in Vietnam, and it appeared that George McGovern, the Democratic candidate, had no issue to counter with.

Scott tilted back in his chair, the better to observe the twin columns of the new World Trade Center. Newspapers said the new north tower leased much of its space already. The upper floors of the south tower still looked raw and ragged, but – from the bottom up – that building too began to fill. People wanted to work there. Gray clouds magically parted as they neared the twin spires. Bright vents of sun beamed through.

Monica Corbin breezed into Scott's office, Barry in tow. "I take my brokerage test in five weeks. Guys, you'd better start looking."

"Pretty confident, aren't you?" Barry said.

"Come on. I'm going to knock it dead."

"Let's call the Swedish Information Center and see if they have young lingerie models who want to learn the brokerage business," Scott said.

"How about a weightlifter who's good with numbers," Barry said.

Monica laughed with them. They had grown comfortable together, the three of them, despite her liaison with the Golden Falcon.

Jennifer waited in the lobby of her apartment building Friday, absorbed in a newspaper. "Miss Cohen, you're wanted in the north," Scott announced himself.

"So, Killington," Jennifer said in the car.

"I hiked up Superstar. It curves, it plunges. It's one of my favorite ski trails."

"I thought people drove up to New England to spin cloth, make cheese. I'm kidding, I'm kidding."

Scott chuckled. He talked about the stock market. "I'm telling my customers to buy before the election, sell the day after."

"It's the old buy on expectation, sell on the news gambit," Jennifer said.

General Brands had promoted her. Nine people reported to her now. Calmly, she discussed office politics and her latest packaging strategies while Scott tussled with rush-hour traffic on the West Side Highway.

"...and then I left my sunglasses at the supermarket and my answering machine broke." Jennifer touched a finger to Scott's nose. "You're handsome, do you know that? Do you plan on going to those auditions again?"

"I think about it. But I told the agency not to call me any more. If somebody stopped me on the street and said, 'Hey, we want to pay you a lot of money to appear in our new silver streak office duplicating machine commercial,' I suppose I'd do it."

"I wish you would. I want to snap on the set and see you."

"I do miss that side of it, the celebrity aspect."

"I never saw the commercial you made for Lancer – phallic name, huh? Do you have a tape of it or a film or anything?"

"I don't," Scott said. "It's probably lost to the ages."

They crossed the Tappan Zee Bridge, jetted north on the Interstate and turned west in the shadow of the Schunemunks.

"Considering your four years at Cornell, I guess you know Route Seventeen pretty well," Scott said.

"I guess I do. I calculated I rode in a car between Great Neck and Ithaca something like sixty-two times."

"Guys? Gals? Who did you ride with?"

"Upperclassmen, whenever possible. Mostly men, I suppose."

No surprise there, Scott thought. He experienced a stirring. "What do you say we stop soon? Darkness comes early to these hills. We'll have plenty of time to get there in the morning."

Jennifer gave him a glance. Languidly she crossed and tossed her limbs.

They stayed at a motel they had never seen before and would probably never see again. They got out of the car and Scott liked it that his breath plumed in the cold.

They dined on Maine crab cakes in a restaurant that radiated noise and frontier bustle. Jennifer wiped butter from her mouth. Back in their room she speed-read a report she brought along, wanting to dispense with responsibility early.

Scott clicked channels on the television until he found a weather forecast. "Looks like a brisk one tomorrow." He never tired of these fronts stalking east.

He flung open a window, spread an extra blanket. Jennifer sped from the bathroom in a black nightie and he saw from the way she lifted her arms that she expected to be ravaged. He imagined her undulating toward him, high heels, black stockings...

It rained in the morning. Windshield wipers clicking, they tracked Route 17 across the southern edges of New York's Catskill Mountains, crossing and recrossing a rocky stream. "The Delaware River," Jennifer said.

"Didn't know it began way up here."

"Well, it does." Interstate 81 jetted them around Binghamton and a smaller road pulled them north over long hills spotted with farms. They saw a cafe with big windows on top of a hill near Willseyville and voted to stop for coffee.

Men in baseball caps talked at tables. The voice of Susan Raye burst from a jukebox: "L. A. International Airport, hear the big, jet engines roar. L. A. International Airport, I won't see him any more..."

Scott noted the sugar dish on each table, the calendars on the walls. "A roadside cafe's roadside cafe," he said.

"What does that mean?"

"It's colloquial. It's a saying."

The rain stopped and a thin sun shone through. They drove over a ridge rounded on top like a vast pumpkin and saw the town of Ithaca and the southern curve of Lake Cayuga. A sprawl of buildings, Cornell University, dominated a hill to the right. Jennifer directed Scott toward the football stadium.

With two hours until kickoff, already a lone student in a slicker peddled game programs and a ticket window opened. Scott purchased two seats for the afternoon game.

They parked on campus and walked – he in sweater and light jacket, she in a sheepskin coat. Jennifer pointed out dormitories where once she lived.

"I want to see ivy," Scott said. Cornell belonged to that group of schools known as The Ivy League and he expected old red brick walls and curly, clinging tendrils.

"You want ivy? I'll show you ivy." Jennifer walked him past an old classroom building. "There!" Indeed, a sprig or two did cling to the walls of the mouldering structure.

They inched forward in a cafeteria lunch line at the alumni center while around them old grads in checked coats shouted insults at each other and embraced.

"See anyone you know?" Scott felt wistful.

"I told you, I never went to football games."

"Maybe somebody cerebral slipped through."

"Ha," Jennifer said.

They climbed to seats high in the stadium. Low, dark clouds raced and flags snapped in the wind. Cornell won the coin toss and chose to kick off. A football rose against the November sky.

First play from scrimmage a Dartmouth end caught a sideline pass. "Watch," Scott said, "they'll do that again." Sure enough, a few plays later they did.

"Yes, but the defense almost stopped it that time." Jennifer leaned forward as if interested. Her dark hair spilled over the top of her sheepskin coat and her face looked framed in fleece.

Scott sloshed brandy into paper cups while players down on the field knocked each other down, jumped up, reformed into patterns and knocked each other down again. "It looks choreographed from up here," Jennifer said.

"That's so. Up here you don't feel the fury."

Marching bands strutted at halftime and they descended from the stands to wander around. A cheerleader stood on a bench waving a pom pom, her legs freckled with cold.

They climbed back to their seats and gazed out over the campus. "Autumn," Scott said. Frantic leaves raced on the wind.

The teams sprinted back on the field, players struggled for yards of ground and the earth slowly turned. "'Dying civilizations turn to sport,'" Scott quoted Oswald Spengler. He enjoyed the spectacle, but it bothered him that he did not care who won.

"Oswald Spengler?"

"After the First World War, before the second one, he wrote a book called *Decline of the West*." He hugged Jennifer in her sheepskin coat. She pretended to shy away as if to say, "I don't know this man."

Students milled after the game and old grads searched for friends. Scott rested his arm around his weekend date. "Where to? Some legendary campus watering hole?"

"Away. Let's go someplace I've never been."

East, they decided, into fresh hills, toward central New York, the Catskills and the unknown.

"I've never attended a high school or a college reunion," Jennifer said. "I'm not nostalgic; places I've worked, places I've lived, I don't go back. I don't care if I see them again."

"Well, of course, your dad left when you were young."

She snorted. "If I said I liked yellow balloons instead of red ones, if I complained of headaches on Tuesdays, you'd say, 'Well, of course, your dad left when you were young.'"

"I sense meaning where others don't," Scott said.

"Your parents divorced. Dig into the ramifications of that."

"I have," Scott said, "and here is my conclusion: if my parents had been warm and reassuring I'd be a corporate chieftain. I'd play golf, I'd smoke cigars."

"You're a softie. You're nostalgic, aren't you?"

"Yes, I guess I am," Scott said.

The wind blew leaves across the road and he enjoyed a feeling of racing for shelter, of cold and darkness coming. They chose a motel beyond Oneonta with frost-stunned flowers and a pebbled stream, and they entered their room as if into a warm, inviting cave.

They watched later, at a nearby restaurant, while a man arranged pine logs in a fireplace, struck a match to crumpled newspapers and lighted a fire. "Notice," Scott said, "not many ashes; it must have just turned cold this last week or so."

Jennifer rolled her eyes.

She spotted something on another table. "That's a General Brands container. I hate folksingers, but I dated several. I wonder if I studied too much. You think I missed something in college?"

"Yes," Scott said.

In bed she asked him about his old girlfriends. He mentioned one or two, sensed she was not that interested, and asked her where she saw herself fifteen years from now.

"...Forty years old and having twenty-two people under me? No, I don't see that as the answer. Driving Tracy to gymnastics class, Brandon to Little League, I don't see that as the answer either."

"What do you see as the answer?"

"Have we had this conversation before?"

"I think we have," Scott said. "I don't think we reached any conclusion then, either."

They walked out into a bright, windy Sunday morning and drove east through church-steeple villages toward the Catskill Mountains. Scott followed the road up Black Dome Valley to its end and parked at a trailhead in the trees. They kicked upward through wet leaves.

Sunlight filtered in dusty beams through a stand of evergreens. "The sacred grotto," Jennifer said.

They climbed Acra Point, the northernmost pinnacle in these mountains, and gazed out at the Hudson River Valley. The river looped, straightened, disappeared and reappeared behind a panorama of knolls and ridges. "The Hudson. Will we ever be done with that accursed stream?" Scott jested.

They lunched on sandwiches they purchased in the last town. A few miles south Thomas Cole, Black Dome and Blackhead Mountains humped shoulder to shoulder. The great, Eastern forest rolled away.

"I've something to tell you," Jennifer said. "I misled you about last weekend. A college friend did visit, but it was earlier, during the week. Remember the weekend we went our different ways, me to Amagansett, you to Davis Park?

"Yes, yes. I remember."

"I met someone in Amagansett that weekend and I've seen him several times since."

"Do I know this person?" Scott tried to act casual.

"His name is Jeffrey Essen and he's an investment banker. He owns a house in East Hampton and last weekend I guested there."

"You stayed at his place?"

"Yes," Jennifer said.

Why do you tell me now?"

"I don't know." She began to cry. "I'm crying," she said.

"Is he Jewish?" Scott asked.

"No, he's Dutch." She actually smiled.

They started down the mountain and Jennifer walked in front. Scott stumbled on a root. "Is it a competition now or have you decided?" he asked.

"My whole history is jumping out of relationships. I'm trying to deal with that," Jennifer said.

Scott considered whether to act angry and decided that it would only waste time. "You don't want to see me any more?"

"I do. I do want to see you, but you are entitled to know there's also this other guy."

"Will you ration your weekends? I mean, how's this going to work?"

"I don't really know. You might meet someone else yourself. Couldn't we just sort of feel our way?"

Scott wondered if the mistake he made at work somehow contributed to this. The Bruce Stantons and Jeffrey Essens of this world don't trade without authorization. "Was there a turning point?" he asked.

"What if I said I was afraid we were getting too close?"

"A turning point. There's always a turning point."

"I met Jeffrey. He asked me out, if you want to call that a turning point."

"He's got a house in East Hampton? Does it front on the ocean?"

"It does, but those things don't matter to me."

"Sure." Now Scott did feel angry.

❖   ❖   ❖

CHAPTER 33

Dr. Michael Cohen, Jennifer's father, called. "You still interested in running in the wind to Newport?" The two stocks Scott Lehmann had recommended to him, National Computer and Intergraphics, continued to do well.

"Ah, yes," Scott said, "it's that time of year."

"We ought to do it soon, before the weather turns cold. Do you and Jennifer have plans this weekend?"

Scott hesitated. "Have you talked to Jennifer lately?"

"Not for a while," the doctor said.

"Why don't you discuss it with her," Scott said. "I'm ready if she is."

They had parted in anger Sunday. Scott waited before he telephoned her, allowing her father time to talk to her first. Now, on Tuesday, he saw her father's invitation as a chance to reconcile with at least a dash of dignity.

He reached Jennifer at her office. "I just talked to my father," she said. "I told him I can't go sailing. Jeffrey asked me out to his house this weekend and I think I want to go."

"Did you tell your dad that?"

"I said I had other plans." Normally calm, she sounded flustered.

"He planned on this, I'm sure he wonders what happened."

"He's my dad, Scott. Leave it to me."

"He's my customer, and I need to talk to him about the market from time to time. Tell him something, for god's sakes."

"I'll tell him when and what I want, okay?"

So they left it. Scott watched yellow-green numbers skitter past on his computer screen and tried to picture Jeffrey Essen. Confident and blond rose to mind, considering the Teutonic sound of the name. Scott visualized a blocky, cocky person in the private-school Bruce Stanton tradition. Throw in handsome, knowing Jennifer. She was not one to launch redemptive social projects.

She called back in an hour. "I told my father that we, not I, had other plans, but that maybe we would like to sail to Newport with him in the spring. Talk to him about stocks whenever you want to. Buy. Sell. I don't care." She hung up.

At least she didn't tell her dad about the other guy. This seemed a plus. Scott decided to take showers, eat breakfast, live as usual. Give this new guy a chance to wear out his welcome.

He wanted openness at lunch time and almost galloped to the Battery. Coolness blew from New York Harbor and he found a bench facing the sun. He stretched his arms, closed his eyes, feeling the sun on his face. Old people sat around him on other benches, eyes closed, intent, faces lifted. That's me someday, Scott thought.

He thought of his parents. It had been nearly a year since he had seen them. How long since he had called? Here's something he could do to take his mind off Jennifer. He returned to his office and telephoned his mother in Illinois.

"Do come see me," she said. "Autumn's a fine time of year."

Scott called his father. "Dad, how about I take you out to dinner this weekend?"

Now he had to go. Several days later, with the help of an efficient Tuttle, Osborn & Durkin travel person who wrangled him a standard-fare ticket, Scott gazed down from an airplane at the sunset shadow of Central Illinois' terminal moraine.

His mother, tall, in her early fifties, waited at Greater Peoria Airport. She left her motor vehicle office early to drive across the prairie to greet him and her five-year-old Buick smelled of cigarettes. "You look tired, Scott," she said.

"It's good to see you, Mother." They drove away from the airport in November early darkness.

"Have you had a freeze yet?" Scott often began by asking about the weather.

"I don't think so. The impatiens are still blooming." His mother wore pearls and a flowered skirt instead of the pants suit he expected. She had recolored her hair, black last time, to a refreshing reddish-brown.

"Where do you put the impatiens, down beneath the dogwood?"

"Yes, in the shade," his mother said. "Impatiens don't like direct sun."

"Did I see you limping, Mother?"

"It's nothing, a little arthritis in my left ankle; too much tennis, the doctor says. I play doubles with the girls."

"Good, I'm glad you exercise. Do you take anything for your ankle?"

"Clinoril, a little, yellow pill, one after breakfast and one after supper."

They drove south through windbreaks of trees and flat, ordered fields. Scott noted and commented on corn shocks, pumpkins, wooden wagons. "I spotted the glacial moraine coming in," he said. "It sits out there all alone."

"I guess your father knows you're coming."

"I take him to dinner tomorrow night. Do you ever see him?"

"We meet each other downtown, we say 'hello.' He talks about retiring to Arizona. I still think about going into the Peace Corps."

"Age doesn't matter, right? I'm sure you could." Whenever his mother talked about the Peace Corps, Scott made it a point to encourage. "It would be an experience, a special experience," he said.

"I could do it financially. I could rent the house for income."

"You could rent the upstairs rooms separately. You could rent them for extra income right now."

"I don't like the idea of somebody up there, and I don't need the money since I paid off the mortgage."

"I know," Scott said, "but I thought maybe, for extra income..."

"I don't understand why your father never bought real estate; he could have done so well. He rents the Erickson house, you know. He always had a trauma about owing money." His mother shook a cigarette from the pack on the dashboard and punched at the automatic lighter. "I smoke at work, but I don't smoke at home."

"How are things at the motor bureau?"

"I sit at a desk, I'm off my feet; I'm happy as long as they don't make me give out license plates."

An Illinois car drove in front of them. "Illinois, Land of Lincoln," its license plates proclaimed. Scott liked that. Abraham Lincoln with his seamed, sad face had remained through the years his enduring American hero. Other icons tarnished, but the old rail splitter held his own.

"It's like a great inland sea, isn't it Mother?" Scott recalled driving west with his parents as a kid and seeing the Rocky Mountains for the first time. At first he thought they were clouds.

His mother watched the road, still wearing her sunglasses though darkness came on. "Romance?" Scott always wanted to ask, but never did. "I'm taking you to dinner tonight," he said.

"Well, thank you, but I made the tomatoes you like and the ham's in the oven. You can take the car later if you want to drive around and see some of your friends."

"Thanks, I might. Tomorrow I'll drive over to see dad."

"I know he will be happy to see you," his mother said.

They passed farm roads where Scott parked with girls in high school, heater humming, radio on, running down the batteries of his old cars. He saw across the flat fields the blinking red light on the water tower of his little town.

"Whatever happened to Barbara Noble, Mother?"

"I don't know where they went. They moved away a year or two after you left."

The two stoplights on Main Street swayed in the breeze. The railroad station now functioned as a restaurant and a fast food place replaced the movie theater. "The old home town," Scott said.

He climbed the stairs to his boyhood room. Tattered sports magazines and his blue stamp album aged on the shelves. He stood for a minute, looking out the window, and descended the stairs. "Want a drink, Mother?"

"Not just now, but you have one."

Scott sat on the front porch with a bourbon and water while she prepared dinner. Streetlights cast their glow, the air felt soft for November. Somewhere he smelled burning leaves. A man passed in a pickup truck and stuck his hand out and waved.

"It's on the table," his mother called.

She served creamed corn, ham, a salad, stewed tomatoes with dumplings and tapioca pudding. His mother could always cook; Scott and his father took that for granted, he realized now. The meals always tasted good and appeared on time.

She picked at her plate. "Take the car as long as you like."

Scott searched the telephone book and called Sandra Ollenbach's house. Her mother answered. "Scott Lehmann, I'll declare. Sandra married, she's in Chicago, I know she will be sorry to have missed you. Please say hello to your mom, and I'll tell Sandra you called."

He considered calling Bill Fosse, the condo speculator who on his recent visit to New York regaled him with victory stories, but decided not to on the grounds that they had already skimmed the conversational cream. He drove his mother's car up and down Main Street and walked in the diner, hoping to see someone he knew.

"How's it going?" called the man behind the counter.

"Can't complain," Scott said.

"What can I get you?"

"Coffee to go." Scott returned to the house, stared at the ceiling in his bedroom and tried not to wonder what Jennifer Cohen did tonight. He joined his mother downstairs and they watched several programs on television.

Scott ran twenty laps – five miles – around the high school football field in the morning. He eyed the empty yard lines and ran forty-yard sprints out on the grass. He had scored touchdowns here. How many teams, how many players, had come and gone since then? Did it matter? It all seemed so important then, but then you realize that new teams and new faces just keep coming.

Scott walked after breakfast to the corner where his father sold farm equipment. He saw his dad, leading a customer around among the tractors, and he paused on the sidewalk, unannounced, to watch.

My god, I do look a little like him, he realized.

The customer laughed, his father must have made a joke. He wore thick-soled shoes and bounced on the balls of his feet and Scott noticed that though his stomach sagged he still had a bushy head of hair. A good omen for me, he thought.

"How you doing, Dad?"

"Scott, good to see you. This is my son," his father said to the customer. Even now, those words had a special ring.

"Finish up, Dad. I'll go kick some tires."

The customer climbed on a tractor seat. His father pointed out levers and gears. Scott remembered hearing his father tell how he casually drove 500, 600 miles a day on the two-lane roads of the fifties, west to Colorado, south to the Ozarks, simply to go and do. What did he want now? Did he look at maps? Did he dream?

His dad made the sale and walked the customer to the office to do the paperwork. He came out and lifted a hand as the man drove away. "You must be happy," he said to Scott. "Seems this stock market only knows one direction, up."

"We'll see what happens after the election." Scott touched a "SOLD" sign on a shiny tractor. "Looks like folks are buying here too."

"You know me. I'm always running scared. Come on. Got some donuts inside."

They sat in scarred chairs beneath a calendar picture of a deer drinking from a mountain pool. His father fingered his right ankle. "Arthritis. Sprained it again last summer."

"Mother's got it too. What do you take for yours?"

"Twelve aspirin, every day."

"Twelve, that seems a lot. She takes clinoril, one after breakfast, one after supper. She says it works. She says she still plays tennis."

"Where does she play tennis?"

"At the club, I think."

A potential customer appeared and his father bounded forth. He showed the man a snow plow attachment and a $20,000 cultivator. The customer left, Scott's dad rubbed his hands. "Son, I'm taking you to dinner at The Gables. That's the new restaurant in the old railroad station. People talk about it, city people come through and praise the food."

"Sounds good, but this one's on me, Dad."

"Not tonight. No, sir, I insist." They rode to The Gables in his father's big car. The older man pointed to gauges over the dashboard that calibrated outdoor temperature and wind direction. They turned a corner and there was the restaurant, a short ride. Scott remembered that even as a young man his father would take his car rather than walk a block.

The restaurant owners served drinks behind the former railroad station's ticket counter. "Give me two for Cincinnati," Scott kidded the bartender.

"I guess you're staying in your old room," his father said. "Would you believe it? Your mother heats with oil on the first floor and wastes electric heat upstairs. It doesn't make any sense at all. She spends and spends on that old house. Old hulks like that just chew you up."

"You ought to tell her that, Dad."

"You think she would listen?"

"Why not? Maybe she thinks you don't want to talk to her."

"Did she say that?"

"No," Scott said, "but I think she'd appreciate your opinion. I think she's embarrassed to ask people about financial things." He had tried for years to trick his parents back together and now he knew it would never happen, but he still did it, out of habit. He wondered if they saw through him all along.

They ordered another round of beers. A young couple entered and nodded as they passed. "You ever hear from Suzanne?" his father asked. Scott brought bosomy Suzanne home for a weekend from college and his father still remembered and asked about her.

"She's in San Diego, we exchange Christmas cards. Speaking of...?"

"Well, you know. I get out occasionally."

"Anyone special?"

"I don't think I want to settle down again. How do you get to the airport tomorrow?"

"Mother's driving."

"If it's not convenient for her, give me a call."

"I will. Thanks."

His father sat quiet for a minute. Scott knew what was coming. "You still like the city?"

"Sometimes I think about leaving," Scott said.

"I get offers for the business," his father said. "You never know. If the market turns sour..."

"Dad, in all honesty, it's not likely." They had covered all this before. "Lehmann and Son," his father envisaged. He talked of it often in earlier days.

His father stopped two blocks from his former wife's house and Scott got out. "Come visit me in the city," Scott said. "I'll get tickets for a Yankee game."

"The Mets maybe. Not those goddamn Yankees." His father was a Chicago White Sox fan.

Scott walked past the Lutheran Church and glanced at the graveyard where someday his parents would lie. He found his mother in the living room reading a magazine. "He took you to The Gables? I hear that's where he always goes."

"Have you been there? You ought to try it, Mother."

"I just don't care for that type of food."

Scott noticed a tennis racket in a corner. He brightened. "Did you play tonight?"

"Tomorrow. We play on Sunday afternoons. I'd play week nights too if I wasn't so tired from the motor vehicles bureau." She laughed. "You think it's too late for me to turn pro?"

"Mother, did you know dad's got arthritis in his ankles just like you?"

"Really?" She leaned forward, almost joyful.

"I told him you have it too. I told him you take clinoril. He said he takes twelve aspirins a day."

"Twelve aspirin! That's ridiculous. That's got to be terrible for his stomach."

"Someone ought to tell him about clinoril."

His mother darted him a glance. "Well, that's what doctors are for."

In bed that night Scott tried to remember: had there been a turning-point, a special quarrel, some moment they all could now look back on, that presaged his parents' separation? He had asked both his parents this question and neither could remember a specific incident.

CHAPTER 34

Richard Nixon won the 1972 Presidential election and Wall Street celebrated. Some talked of the Dow Industrials at 1,500, or even 2,000, within 10 or 20 years.

Scott Lehmann and Brent Hall attacked a platter of steamer clams in a restaurant off Sheridan Square. "I've got competition," Scott said. "Jennifer's dating an investment banker."

Brent put down his fork. "Jennifer Cohen?"

Scott nodded. It was dark outside, cold winds lashed Greenwich Village, and he and Brent had played basketball at the Leroy Street gym. They sat indoors, rather than at one of the outdoor tables, for only the second time since spring.

Brent looked thoughtful. "Does she sleep with you both?"

Scott poured himself a glass of sangria. "I'm not sure if I'm still in the rotation or not."

"I'm sorry to hear this," Brent said. "What I mean is, I'm sorry if you're sorry."

"His name is Jeffrey Essen. I wonder if Jennifer ever mentioned him to Ruth. Do she and Jennifer still talk, do you know?"

"I don't think they've talked lately," Brent said. "If they did, Ruth would tell me. Did this guy just ride in out of the mists?"

"Jennifer met him in East Hampton about a month ago. He owns a house out there. It appears he and I played dueling weekends on and off through October."

"What does he look like?"

"I don't know. I haven't met him."

"Essen? What kind of name is that?"

"Jennifer says he's Dutch." Scott played with his glass. "Tuttle, Osborn and Durkin plans to open an office in Jackson Hole, Wyoming. You've seen *Shane*? The magnificent Tetons? That's Jackson Hole country. There's a ski area too."

Brent stared at him. "Oh for Christ's sake. Now you want to leave New York?"

"It's not a new idea. I've thought about it before."

"You won't find women milling about in Jackson Hole like you do on Fire Island. Well – except maybe during ski season. Not like those sixishes, though. Besides, you leave, you lose all your customers. Nobody in the Bronx wants a broker in Wyoming."

"You'd transfer your account to Wyoming. Wouldn't you?"

"Would I?" Brent seemed to consider.

"I'd have to rebuild my book, that's true," Scott said. "I'd have to cold call ranchers and chat up wranglers." Sitting here, drinking sangria in Sheridan Square, the idea of moving to Wyoming did seem far fetched. But he seriously considered it last night; it seemed entirely feasible then.

Brent leaned in, narrowed his eyes, lowered his voice. "I know men who moved to obscure but beautiful places to hunt and fish and travel, to finally do the things they said they had waited all their lives to do. They left the city. They bought cabins with views. Within three weeks they wanted their old jobs back."

"Sure," Scott said, "you knew a lot of guys like that."

"Quite a few," Brent nodded, "quite a few."

"Maybe it's my Charlie Russell painting," Scott said. "It's there in front of me, every day."

"Well, yes; and you're into skiing and hiking and all that."

"It's not just Jennifer. Truth is, I've thought about breaking free from the city for quite a while now. I thought about it in the Adirondacks, I thought about it on Fire Island. "

"I've always wanted to take a year off and go to Europe," Brent said. "You've heard me talk about it."

"You could, you and Ruth."

"Not now. She's pregnant. That was going to be my big announcement tonight."

Scott stared at him. "A kid," he said. "Little basketballs."

"Ivy League catalogs."

"'Dad, can I borrow the car?'" They were off and running. "I'm feeling better," Scott said.

Brent leaned in, a crafty look in his eye. "You can ace this Jeffrey what's-his-name."

"He's a partner in his firm. He owns a beach house."

"Yes, but who gets tickets to the right Broadway shows?"

"He does," Scott said. But Brent stirred his competitive instincts.

They played with possibilities, mentioning the right books, wearing black, things Scott might do to glide Jennifer back into his arms.

Walking home, Scott gave a dollar to a vagrant bundled against the cold. Restless in his apartment, he considered how he might become a more exciting person. Brood in public? Let his hair grow?

Next day, as if by divine intuition, Jeanette from the actors' agency called him at his office. "You're right for this, Scott. It's a beer commercial and it's big bucks. They want two men in their twenties. Residuals could run to ten or twenty thousand. Audition tomorrow morning on Lexington Avenue. They call in a crowd and it's a long shot, but what the hey?"

Talk about timing; Scott might have rejected this out of hand a month ago. But now... He pictured backslaps at the office, Jennifer turning on her television...

"Tell me when and where again."

Scott asked Barry and Monica to say, if anyone asked, that he had an appointment with a client. Next morning, after a quick breakfast, he caught a cab uptown.

Hopefuls clogged the agency office. A young woman wearing bib overalls handed him a sheet of three lines to practice. Scott read them through: "Oh yeah?" "Watch me catch her attention."

"Told you." His turn came, he faced the camera and tried to deliver his words in an arresting, quixotic way.

"Again, please."

This is sheer shit, Scott thought. But it pays well. They had him do it three times.

Jeanette called him at his office an hour later. "They liked you. They want you back."

Scott told Monica that tomorrow he wore jeans and a short-sleeved shirt to his audition, and that then he would change and arrive at the office before noon.

"This is exciting. Good luck," she said.

He carried office clothing with him – suit, shirt, tie – and mussed his hair. He counted only six other male contenders at the callback. "Try it with Tony," the casting director said.

Tony led, Scott responded, they each read three lines. The casting director scratched her chin. "Scott, right? do the other lines this time. Feel it. You two are hanging out on the street. Here comes the world's sexiest woman."

Scott had not practiced the other part but he felt sufficiently into the spirit of the thing. This time he spoke first and the other actor responded. They imagined the woman approaching.

Scott: "Betcha can't."

Tony: "Oh yeah?"

Scott: "She's walking by."

Tony: "Watch me catch her attention." He cocked his head and looked her up and down. Here, in the commercial, the woman stops and smiles at him.

Scott: "Bingo!"

Tony (aside): "Told you."

The casting director: "Good. We'll let you know."

Scott hurried to his office, Jeanette called around three. "Sorry, friend, they took the two scuzziest. They liked you. They said they want look at you again on something else."

"'Scuzziest?' Is that your term, Jeanette?"

"They took the two youngest. Now they tell me. They wanted college kids."

"There wasn't anybody there under twenty-five," Scott said.

"I'll put your pictures out again." She read from a list of upcoming campaigns.

"No, Jeanette," Scott heard himself say. "Thanks anyway. I guess I'll become a full-time broker now."

He paced around his office, surprised at himself. "Scott, Mrs. Lander on line two," he heard Monica call.

❖ ❖ ❖

CHAPTER 35

Scott sat in his favorite chair, facing the illuminated Empire State Building, and read notations he had made next to names and telephone numbers in his old, green address book.

"Met at Roger's party." "Westhampton Beach. Cut hand." "Bellringer party, '71" "Art show. Difficult."

There, that last one. His finger nestled in the V's, on Brittany VanHorn, she of the sexy gap between her teeth.

"It's pretty late to call, isn't it, one day in advance? I'm invited to a party, but I suppose... Let me see..."

Scott agreed to pick her up at her apartment tomorrow at seven. They had met in June at an art exhibition sponsored by ZaneCorp. Now, in early December, he had tickets for a similar show sponsored by an oil company in a mansion on Fifth Avenue.

He strolled East Sixty-First Street to Brittany VanHorn's apartment. He loved this block, its soft lights, its trees, its brownstones. Brittany wore a black dress and she looked good, same farm-girl wide shoulders, same wheat field hair.

"My boss asked me to accompany him to Puerto Rico." He glimpsed the moist crevice between her teeth.

"Your boss is married?"

"He says his wife is married, but he isn't."

"Don't I remember a married tennis instructor who yearned to whisk you away?"

Brittany swung an imaginary racquet. "I don't take from him anymore."

They examined, at the art exhibit, splashes of red and yellow bisected by streaks of blue and green. Many of the paintings looked like cartoons, she said. Scott agreed.

They browsed a buffet and descended to a basement disco on East Eighty-Sixth Street. Brittany danced as she talked, positioning one leg, rocking to the other, forcing reactions. Between dances they talked at a table. She described her father as a ne'er do well and her mom as a put-upon widow in Hackensack. She told him again how she fought her younger brother's battles. She worked still as a paralegal, and next year she hoped to go to law school.

"Good for you. I considered law school myself. In fact, a friend of mine just started at NYU." Scott passed on Art Levin's first-year impressions. He risked a rhyme: "Island village, Indian forts; serious students joust with torts."

Brittany nodded to the words of his poem as if Scott hopped from rock to rock. The gap between her teeth glistened. "You thought about law school? Why didn't you do it?"

"I decided I like being a stockbroker." Should he mention his trading-without-authorization scandal? No. He asked her to dance.

They left the disco a little before midnight. Winter impended and naked tree limbs in the East Eighties stretched like nerves against the sky. They walked south down Second Avenue and east on Sixty-First past little metal balconies and gingerbread-house doors.

Brittany asked him up and they climbed an outer and then an inner set of stairs. She put on music, kicked off her shoes, sat beside him. "Were you ever engaged to be married?" she asked.

"Close once or twice," Scott said. "What about you?"

"No. Nyet. Nein. I was asked, several times. I'm in no hurry." She pulled up her knees and her dress tightened about her thighs.

"You look especially good tonight, Brittany." He leaned carefully toward her.

"Thank you. Is that the doorbell?"

"I didn't hear anything."

She cocked an ear. "I guess you're right." He kissed her and they slid lower on the couch, touching, embracing.

Scott remembered how she went this far and no further back in June and he determined this time to show patience. She pulled away and looked at him. "I hope you understand. I don't want to go all the way until I'm married."

"Go all the way." Scott mulled the phrase in his mind. It had been a while since he had heard it. "Understood," he said.

He met her in midtown a few days later. It was Wednesday night and already dark and snowflakes skittered. Brittany wore boots and a fluffy coat. They idled up Fifth Avenue and down Madison amid a chorus of Christmas bells, stopping at display windows to look at department stores' holiday decorations.

They dined at a restaurant she liked, strolled around some more and returned to her apartment. He touched with his tongue the moist gap between her teeth.

"Whoops!" they tumbled down on the rug. She lay on her back and he slid down, grasped her wrists and lifted them – standard procedure with Jennifer – to open the way.

"What are you doing!" She jerked herself up.

"I thought..."

"You tried to force me!"

Perhaps he had. Why? Did he look for an excuse to break away? In truth, he realized, he had given her no chance at all. He had played Mr. Cool from the beginning. Maybe if he left now, returned another day and started over. Maybe if he credited her for making her way in a tough world.

"It's late," he said, hoping she would suggest he stay.

"And tomorrow's a work day," she said.

Scott considered on the subway. Who else did he want to date? Run the list, he thought, do it now. He called Marlene Miller in the morning at the ad agency where she worked. Barry Kalish had recommended a new disco, The Dragon's Tit. Marlene said she was free Friday night.

This left Saturday open and Scott telephoned Brittany VanHorn. He apologized for past foolishness and asked her out Saturday night. She thanked him for apologizing but said she she was going to New Jersey this weekend to visit her mother.

Marlene Miller lived on West End Avenue two blocks from the Hudson River. Her summer tan somehow lingered into December and Scott warmed at the sight of her. She looked tall and stunning in her black jumpsuit.

"You wore that last summer to the sixish. I'll not forget."

"Close. I wore it dancing at The Casino, actually."

He flagged a cab. Their knees touched in the back seat. "Do you still see Jennifer, the one you bought out to the house?"

"Not lately. How about you and The Tennis Player?"

"We talk." She waggled her hands. "So. How are you?"

"Fine. I keep thinking we just came from the beach, and now we're on our way to the Casino."

"Did Larry Silverman call you about coming into the house next summer?"

"He did," Scott said. "I don't know yet. Art Levin will come back, I think. He's dating Barbara Feldstein. You heard? That complicates things. Do they return to the house together? What if they have a fight or want to turn celibate or something?"

"I think Barbara will guide them through somehow," Marlene said.

"What about you, Marlene? What will you do next summer?"

"I told Larry I haven't made up my mind. I know people in a house in East Hampton and I might join there. I wouldn't miss those long ferry rides out to Fire Island."

"Yes, but...there's something special about crossing Great South Bay."

"Like leaving civilization," Marlene said.

They arrived at the disco. They ordered drinks. "The Dragon's Tit." Marlene rolled the words.

"Wouldn't want to get pinched in here," he said. She chuckled, that deep laugh he remembered.

Scott observed, as he and Marlene danced, that she caught mens' eyes over his shoulder, as she did back at the Casino. Of course he knew he played the same game.

They danced until late, caught a cab and she invited him up. She poured glasses of orange juice and they sat on a couch next to each other.

"Arnold's dating a blonde, a shiksa," Marlene said. "I think it's just a phase." She didn't need to explain. Scott knew she referred to The Tennis Player.

"Jennifer's seeing a male shiksa, an investment banker."

"Serious?"

"I don't know. I hope I'm still in the game."

Marlene kicked off her shoes. Scott studied her reflection in a mirror; full lips, brown eyes, long legs. "Want music?" she asked.

"Not now," he said. "Do you ever think of waves pounding in below the Casino, dancing to Aretha Franklin, hiding your drinks behind the jukebox?"

"I think of the sun and beach and wondering who I'm going to meet tonight," Marlene said. She brought out some marijuana and they each smoked.

"Yes," Scott said, watching a red fruit bowl on a table begin to simmer, "the colors come alive."

He stared at her legs, his glance lingered. He saw her expression change.

He put down his orange juice. "One for the road?" he asked.

"Why not?" She rose and he followed her into her bedroom. They writhed together. It seemed almost incestuous, all the sweeter because unplanned.

"I won't tell if you don't," Marlene said.

CHAPTER 36

Scott Lehmann parked near Jennifer Cohen's building Saturday morning and jogged into Central Park. It was a soft, sunny day, surprisingly warm for this late in the year. He had the strange feeling that Jennifer also jogged nearby, and that he would meet her at the stone fortress on the south side of the reservoir.

He trotted around the water, picturing her waiting and watching for him. Maybe she had also waited on other days. He imagined her turning away, frowning, disappointed when he did not come.

But he did not see her at the stone fortress so he kept going and passed the same spot two more times. He ran for two hours, seeking that giddy, spent state, that antidote against woe, that running or long-distance hiking will sometimes produce. Peace, though, did not descend.

What the hell, he thought. He looked for a pay phone and telephoned her apartment.

"Scott." She did not sound surprised.

"Want to go jogging?" It seemed an innocuous proposal, one to which she might without guilt or rancor respond.

"Actually, I think I would," she said. "I'm sure you heard: National Computer made a tender offer for Intergraphics yesterday. Jeffrey's bank is involved in the negotiations and he's in San Diego."

"I've got customers in both stocks," Scott said. "Some are happy, some are not." Intergraphics rose and the suitor, National Computer, declined, as was usually the case after tender offers. "Which side is Jeffrey on?"

"The aggressor, naturally."

"Why 'naturally'? He's ruthless by nature?"

"Yes. No. I don't know. I've done nothing but sit this week and I need exercise. I'll meet you at the stone house at two-thirty."

She waited in an orange jogging suit. Her hair looked interestingly longer, though it had only been a few weeks. Scott kissed her, slightly off center, a cousin's kiss. She tasted faintly of sweat. He did not mention his earlier run while they loped three laps around the reservoir, thus pushing his total to over 12 miles for the day.

He was young. He felt good. He told her about his trip to see his parents and they talked of work and the election. "It's still early," she said. "Want to stop by?"

"I'd like that. I brought a change of clothes in my car."

"Lucky guess." She made it easy for him.

The doorman recognized him and nodded. Scott toted his regular clothes in a gym bag, the same he used when he played basketball, and they rode up the silent elevator. He showered and changed and Jennifer followed him into the bathroom and stepped forth in a white blouse, dark skirt and shiny shoes.

"You took your time calling," she said. She handed him a bottle of red wine to open.

"I experimented, I dated other women."

"How did that go?"

"Possibilities..." They stepped out on her terrace. Last leaves still idled along the sidewalks below. Buildings on Fifth Avenue across Central Park glinted like Antarctic cliffs in the low December sun.

"You ought to speak to the super about putting a shield up to protect your guests from this view," Scott said.

Jennifer started to object and smiled when she realized he kidded.

"I talked to your dad Thursday. He bought some stock. Apparently he thinks we're still entangled, and I did not tell him different."

"I haven't told him otherwise," Jennifer said.

"I must have run forty miles today," Scott said, "hoping to see you."

"Funny, I had feeling you might wander by." She lifted her shiny shoes to the terrace railing. "What are you reading?"

"*On the Road.*"

"Again?"

"I go back to what I enjoy. How about you?"

"*Mansfield Park*," Jennifer said. "Jane Austen makes Fanny and Edmund such prudes I find myself rooting for the Crawfords. I think Jane Austen liked the Crawfords best."

"You and Jane Austen. That's not a combination I would have expected."

"Why not? You forget. I read it because you recommended it."

"That's right; I guess I did. Want to eat at that place on Columbus Avenue?"

"Yes," she said. "I think I pointed out that Jeffrey's out of town."

It was December dark when they descended the elevator. Scott and the doorman nodded at each other. Good times, bad times, he thought, these guys always seemed on his side.

They pressed their noses against the restaurant window, reading tonight's specials, imprinting little circles of breath fog. They entered and someone called to Jennifer from across the room. "That's Amy from work, I'll go over for a minute, okay?"

Scott got a table. Jennifer returned. "She wants to transfer to media. She doesn't want to run the copier ever again."

"Can you solve her problem?"

"I think so." She squared her shoulders. "Did you miss me, Big Fellow?"

"I did."

"But you dated some?"

"Some."

"That was an idiotic thing you did, buying stock without permission, but mon pere wants us to ride the winds to Newport with him in the spring. You got him all fired up about that. I'm happy to see him fired up about anything."

"What about the house on the beach at East Hampton?"

"First time, exciting. Third time... Jeffrey's more settled than you, I think. He's more predictable."

"That's good?"

"Sometimes, like when you're planning a life. Other times..."

"You want coffee?" Scott asked.

"I don't care."

"I don't. I'll ask for the check when we finish."

"I looked at the new skis this week," Jennifer said.

"Is Jeffrey a skier?"

"I don't think so."

"Did you buy the skis?"

"Yes."

A blustery wind assaulted them outside. Jennifer gripped his arm and they sailed down Central Park West. She opened her apartment door. She plunked down her keys and in the flow of that motion Scott guessed what was coming. They shed their clothes. He kissed her nipples. He petted her silken muff. He carried her toward the bedroom and the rug beneath his bare feet felt eight inches thick. Jennifer dropped her arm, kerplunk, across the bed.

She fought and kicked. He forced her legs apart and she swung them high. He slid between. She bucked and reared and screamed at the end.

They lay quietly in a dark room ten floors above Central Park. "You do these things with other women?"

"Not really," Scott said. "I don't know what it is with you."

"I guess you have to have the right receptors. I fantasize when you hold me down, you know."

"A uniform? A monocle?"

"Tall strangers from outer space. I'm kidding, I'm kidding. Actually, short sleeves, muscles, maybe a scar."

"Is there a face?" Scott asked.

"Indistinct. Heavy eyebrows."

"Me?"

"I don't know."

"I found a parking spot that's good 'till morning." Scott said.

"You might as well stay over then," Jennifer said.

❖   ❖   ❖

CHAPTER 37

Scott Lehmann and Art Levin sunned on the steps of the Federal Building. Art had taken a test on contracts that morning and had the rest of the day free. "Larry Silverman called," he said. "We're supposed to send in our deposits for next summer. What about you, Storm?"

"I don't know, Lamont." He did know, but superstitious, not wanting to cast a hex on anything, Scott kept it to himself. He and Jennifer had talked it over and decided to bounce around to different locales next summer.

"If we don't sign up as regulars," he said, "Jennifer and I could dart out from time to time as guests. You could bring Barbara as a guest too, you know. I mean, you both don't have to join."

"Emotions raw, emotions limber; why not sign on as a member?"

"It just too early to decide. That's all."

It felt suddenly colder, and the two of them glanced upward. The sun hung low in this, the final month of the year, and as the day wore on shadows cast by other structures crept higher and higher up the steps of the Federal Building. One of these shadows nipped at their ankles, so the two men slid two rows further up the steps.

"Jennifer and I may move in together," Scott said.

"Holy moly. Big decision, Storm."

"A test. A way to find out."

"Her place, of course. I've seen your apartment."

"True. She's got the better view."

"I remember when the two of you climbed the forbidden mountain. What was it? Mankiller? Widow Maker?"

"Marcy."

The shadow advanced, they moved up two more steps. "What do you want to tell me about law school?" Scott asked.

"I'm on track. Do you wonder about things, Storm? I wonder if twenty years from now I'll wind up in one of those grubby little offices on East Forty-Second Street, suing some restaurant owner because plaster fell from a ceiling into somebody's soup."

Scott laughed. "Christ. Twenty years. I see myself on the telephone selling something. Dirigibles. Lakefront real estate." He glanced at his watch. "Duty alert."

"Hello to Jennifer."

"Likewise to Barbara."

"Buy low, sell high, Lash Storm."

"Take care, Lamont Gramercy Cranston." Scott glanced back and saw Art lean forward and speak to two young women. A rhyme, he liked to think. He purchased a cup of tea and an apple raisin muffin and carried his lunch up the elevator in a brown paper bag.

Mr. Polinsky called and bought a new stock. Mrs. Lander asked for quotes. Yellow-green numbers skittered across his computer screen.

"The applicant's here," Monica Corbin said.

She had passed her brokerage examination and would soon become a trainee in a Tuttle, Osborn office uptown. A candidate for her sales assistant job had called and Barry had asked him to come in for an interview this afternoon.

A tall, thin young man appeared and introduced himself as Richard. The three of them talked in Barry's office. Richard told a risque story, and referred to his mother several times as "Morganna."

Richard left. "I like him," Barry said.

"He seems totally intolerant of people without money," Scott said.

"No? Is that what you're saying?"

"Yes."

Walter Cappaletti made the final decisions, but would be guided by what Scott and Barry wanted. They agreed to keep looking.

Scott met Brent Hall at the Leroy Street Gym after work and they climbed the metal stairs to the playing floor. A bunch of aging regulars shot baskets at one end. They chased neighborhood kids from the other end and began a game.

Back and forth. Brent had played himself into basketball shape and time seemed to slow as they raced up and down the court. They lost a game and leaned against the wall, watching, impatient to return. Scott felt strong, eager. He could not believe that someday he would be too old.

They stopped for steamers and sangria afterward at the restaurant in Sheridan Square. "You asked her to marry you?"

"It's implied," Scott said. "The plan is to live together. Why do married people always want single people to get married? Is it a share the misery kind of thing?"

"We want you to be happy too," Brent said.

A skim of snow filtered down in the night. Scott called a number in Vermont to check on ski conditions. He and Jennifer had reservations at Stratton for the Christmas holidays. Somebody offered him tickets for a rock concert Friday by a British band, the Moody Blues, and he called Jennifer to confirm.

"I'll pick you up at six thirty."

"What about dinner? Will that give us time?"

"Okay, six fifteen."

Scott gazed out his window at the Empire State Building poking up and out of sight into a low, gray sky. He recalled the flat, shimmering vistas of Central Illinois and regretted that when he visited his parents he did not drive a few miles further to see the glacial moraine. He pictured it now, zinging the flats, a slowly eroding arrow of possibility.

He read a memo extolling Tuttle, Osborn's planned new brokerage office in Jackson Hole and carried the memo into Walter Cappaletti's office. "Just curious, Walter. How will the firm staff this new office in Wyoming?"

"They'll choose a veteran as office manager and fill desks with transfers or new people. A startup like this, you really start from scratch."

"New York still the popular place?"

"Oh yes. I get six, seven applications a week from men and women who want to become brokers in this office." He looked out his window. "This is the place to be."

Scott returned to his desk and noticed that the winter sun slid so low it illuminated his painting of the mountain men. There they were, the three adventurers, riding the high country out in wind and weather, living lives at the glorious edge. Until you run out of bullets, Scott thought. Until a grizzly tears off your arm. Maybe he should replace the painting with a beach scene.

He stepped into Barry Kalish's office, research reports in hand. The Dow Jones had closed above 1,000 and Scott felt pressured to increase his commission business accordingly. "Did Walter speak to you about higher production goals for next year?"

"He did," Barry said. "I wondered if he spoke to you."

"He asked me to up my targets by twenty per cent; I hear that's what he asked everybody."

"If we had wanted easy jobs," Barry said, "we would have gone into the Civil Service."

Scott sat at his desk and gazed at the skyline of New York City silhouetted against a red December sun. He folded his hands and leaned back. There's Jennifer, he thought. There's the ever-moving translucent numbers. But still... He wondered if he would ever hear the voices again.

He watched, mesmerized, as today's closing prices marched across his computer screen.

The End

Made in the USA
San Bernardino, CA
25 June 2013